LONE STAND

Red Denning had his back against a wall. That wall was solid granite, soaring two hundred feet above his head. Arrayed against him more than a dozen men held him pinned down with a steady hail of gunfire. Newly returned from the Civil War, he found his nemesis had turned the country against him. He had been neatly framed for a vicious crime and the woman who promised to wait for him was being pressured by her father to marry Red's worst enemy. As night settled in, his hope of seeing the sunrise rested entirely on the success of his last, desperate plan.

LONE STAND

LONE STAND

by

Billy Hall

Dales Large Print Books
Long Preston, North Yorkshire,
BD23 4ND, England.

British Library Cataloguing in Publication Data.

Hall, Billy
    Lone stand.

    A catalogue record of this book is
    available from the British Library

    ISBN   978-1-84262-651-1 pbk

First published in Great Britain 2007 by Robert Hale Limited

Copyright © Billy Hall 2007

Cover illustration © Gordon Crabb by arrangement with
Alison Eldred International

Published in Large Print 2008 by arrangement with
Robert Hale Limited

Dales Large Print is an imprint of Library Magna Books Ltd.

Printed and bound in Great Britain by
T.J. (International) Ltd., Cornwall, PL28 8RW

CHAPTER 1

'Them's union boots. I hate the sight of them stinkin' shiny things.'

Red Denning glanced at the speaker, but continued toward the bar. His response was soft-spoken. 'They're just what I got.'

From the hand of poker at a round table the first speaker answered. His eyes glinted hard as diamonds from his pinched face. 'Better'n anythin' we ever got,' he growled. 'If'n we'da had the shoes 'n guns you Yankees had, we'da run ya clean back t' Boston where you belonged.'

Red shrugged his broad shoulders and bellied up to the bar. Over his shoulder he said, 'War's over now.' To the bartender he said, 'Got any good whiskey?'

'Nope. Got some fair-to-middlin' stuff, though.'

Red smiled slightly. 'That'll do. Three fingers' worth.'

The bartender set a cloudy glass on the bar and poured a generous measure of whiskey. He took the coin Red had dropped on the bar and nodded his thanks, turning away.

Red sipped the amber liquid, watching the poker table in the mirror behind the bar, without appearing to do so.

The conversation at the poker table continued to get more animated. After several minutes, the bartender moved past Red, speaking softly without being obvious. 'Might watch them two. They been hangin' around town last two-three days. Itchin' for a fight.'

Red murmured an almost inaudible 'Thanks,' as he sipped his drink. The warning was unnecessary, but he appreciated it nonetheless.

The challenge came about when he anticipated. 'What outfit was you with, Yankee?'

Red turned slowly, responding to the challenge he knew was brewing, no matter what he did or said. 'Cavalry unit, under General Gregg.'

'Was ya at Gettysburg?'

'Yeah, I was there.'

'So was we. Pickett's outfit.'

Red made a sympathetic sound with his top lip against his teeth. 'Tough spot to be in. You boys lost a lot of men in that charge.'

'Too many,' the man agreed. 'We'da won, if somebody hadn't spilled our plans.'

Trying to redirect the man's intent, Red asked, 'You stay with Pickett after that?'

The man nodded again. 'Clear through the war, pertneart. All the way ta Five Forks.'

Red grimaced. 'You ended up in all the wrong places.'

''T'ain't that funny.'

'Didn't mean it that way. It was a tough time. We all lost a lot of friends.'

'Lost a lot more'n that. After Petersburg fell, they herded us into pens like cattle. Treated us worse'n any cattle ever was. Spent the whole winter there. Both of us did. Pertneart died twice.'

Red pursed his lips. 'I 'spect you were right. If you boys had been outfitted well, you'd have whipped our tails.'

'Dang right we would've! We're heeled now, though.'

As if that were a signal, both men stood from the table. The one who had remained silent throughout sidled back and to the side, putting a good six feet between himself and his friend.

Red moved half a step away from the bar, letting his hand fall next to the butt of the Russian .44. It wasn't in a military-style holster; it was in a lower cut holster, further down on his leg, the bottom tied to his thigh by a thin strip of leather. No cover hindered access to the well-worn walnut grips.

The Confederate veteran either didn't notice, or had had too much to drink to care.

'You don't want to do this,' Red countered. 'I didn't come in here looking for trouble. The war's over.'

'Not fer us, it ain't. Not so long's even one o' you uppity-up Yankees is still standin'. We got as good a guns as you got, now. Thet, an' they's two of us.'

Others in the saloon had scattered the instant the pair stood. Now they crowded back farther, as if to press back into the rough walls, out of harm's way. Deathly silence settled across the room, making every word audible in the breathlessness of expectation.

'Two isn't enough,' Red said softly. 'Don't push it. I'll finish my drink and be on my way. You can say you ran me out of town, if it'll make you feel better.'

'Not by a dang sight!' the speaker declared, clawing for his gun.

Red had long since assessed the relative danger of the pair. His assessment was right. Before the speaker had even finished his sentence, his wordless partner's gun was out of his holster, lifting toward the hated representative of everything the word 'Yankee' stirred in his heart.

Red's gun appeared as if by magic in his hand, spitting a streak of fire in the dim interior of the saloon. The silent man's grunt

11

as the .44 caliber slug shattered his heart was the first sound he had made. His own gun discharged into the floor, spewing a small cloud of sawdust.

Echoes of the shots hadn't stopped their bounce between clapboard walls before Red's second shot drove the speaker backward. His gun was still not completely clear of leather. Stunned confusion crossed his face. He opened his mouth to speak, but only a fountain of blood issued forth. He fell silently.

Red watched both men carefully for a long moment, assuring himself they were dead. With a long sigh he expelled the two spent casings from the cylinder and replaced them with fresh loads. As if the whole room copied his sigh, a whisper wafted across the room. Then it erupted with excited chatter of a dozen voices.

'Did you see that?'

'Happened so quick I ain't sure what I saw.'

'I seen that one fella practicin' out back yesterday. He was plumb greased lightnin'.'

'Didn't look like it today.'

'Not next t' thet fella. I didn't even see 'im go fer 'is gun. It was jist all of a sudden there, spittin' fire.'

'Didn't know ya could see flame come out've a gun like thet.'

'Me neither. 'Course, I ain't never seen one fired inside like this afore.'

'What was they, three shots? Sounded almost like one long one.'

'Sure warn't no space between 'em, thet's fer sure.'

The chatter was interrupted by somebody bursting through the door. A man with a badge pinned to his vest, carrying a leveled, sawn-off shotgun, stopped just inside the door. His eyes swept the interior in an instant.

'What's goin' on, Jesse?' he demanded.

'It's over, Marshal,' the bartender responded. 'Them two pushed this fella. Tried to make him go for his gun. When he wouldn't, they both did anyway. They weren't anywhere near quick enough.'

13

The marshal eyed Red up and down. 'That the how of it?'

Red nodded. 'I tried to talk 'em out of it. They've been nursing hurts from the war too long to listen, I reckon.'

One of the bystanders piped up, 'He tried two or three times t' tell 'em the war's over. They wouldn't listen.'

Another affirmed it. 'He told 'em that two of 'em wasn't enough, too. They jist wasn't gonna let the war be over.'

'Over for 'em now,' the first bystander observed.

The marshal nodded. 'I guess that's the only way it'll be over for too many on both sides,' he offered.

He turned to Red. 'You got business in town?'

Red shook his head. 'Nope. Just holed up for the night. Got a room at the hotel. Stopped in for a drink.'

'Where ya headed?'

'Wyoming. Got a homestead there I left for the war.'

'Whose outfit was ya in?'

'Gregg's.'

'Cavalry?'

'Yeah.'

'I was with Pickett.'

Red's hand eased closer to his gun butt again. 'Sorry,' was all he could think of to say.

'Bad business,' the marshal said.

'War's always bad business.'

The marshal nodded. 'They oughta make the politicians fight, instead o' honest men.'

'That'd sure shorten the wars.'

'Put an end to 'em, that's what it'd do.'

'That couldn't be all bad.'

'Couldn't be bad at all. Wyoming, huh?'

'Yeah. Up close to Lennox, if you know where that is.'

The marshal shook his head. 'Never been there. Mountain country?'

Red nodded. 'Right at the edge o' the mountains. Good grass. Runnin' water. Cows can graze up into the mountains in summer, an' back down come winter. Don't hardly have to even put up any hay.'

'Sounds good.'

'Peaceful place.'

'All Union folks thereabouts?'

Red shrugged. 'Mostly, I guess.'

'That'll be good. Maybe you won't have any more deals like this one.'

Beginning to relax, Red said, 'I sure hope not. There's been enough killin'.'

It was the marshal's turn to nod agreement. 'Yup, but it won't end fer a good while. Too many men seen an' done too much killin'. Warps their mind. Be a good while afore they either learn t' think straight again or get themselves killed.'

Battlefield scenes flashed across Red's mind. He forced himself to suppress a shudder. All he could trust his voice to say was, 'Yeah.'

The marshal turned to the bartender. 'I'll send Oliver over to get those two and lay them out, in case they have any family that comes looking for 'em.'

The bartender only nodded. The marshal

turned back to Red. More a question than a statement, he said, 'You'll be leaving in the morning?'

Red sighed again. 'No, I'll probably gather up my stuff and head on out tonight. Best if I'm not too available, in case those two have friends or family.'

'Might be wise,' the marshal agreed. 'Good luck with your homestead. Got anybody waitin' for ya?'

A whole different set of memories flashed across Red's mind, eclipsing the traumatic ones in an instant, He smiled slightly. 'Yeah. I 'spect she's waitin'.'

The marshal nodded and turned, leaving without another word. Red finished the drink and followed him out the door, his thoughts a long way away, on far more pleasant subjects.

CHAPTER 2

His eyes swept the scene before him. He inhaled deeply. The smell of grass and wild flowers, pine, spruce and cedar trees, mingled together in the high, clear mountain air, triggered a parade of memories. He smiled quietly.

Spread out below him, the wide valley was lush with deep grass, even this early in the spring. Only on the side hills and hill tops was sage brush dominant. It was almost non-existent across the bottom of the valley, where the grass choked out all of the less desirable vegetation. A mountain stream babbled merrily through the center of the verdant valley, laughing at its own tortuous bends and twists. Its banks were lined with cottonwoods, honey locust and willow trees. Spilling out beyond the trees, wild plum, chokecherry and blackberry bushes gave way at the fringes to clumps of wild roses, nettles, and small brush of half-a-dozen species.

At the head of the valley, the Big Horn Mountains rose majestically into the sky. Their tops gleamed white with snowcap that covered more than the top half this early in the season. Near the head of the valley, a cliff jutted skyward. Strewn with boulders and talus the first third of its height, it then rose perpendicularly more than 200 feet. Elsewhere, the length of the valley, draws and gullies reached back into the surrounding mountains, providing food and cover for deer, elk, moose, mountain lions, bears, and a wide range of smaller animals.

Above it all the impossibly deep blue of the sky was broken only by occasional white, fleecy clouds that only accented the vastness of the blue dome. It was a scene of beauty not matched in any other part of the country.

He sat his horse almost sideways, right leg wrapped around the saddle horn. He rolled himself a smoke from the bag of tobacco in his shirt pocket, lighting it with a match he struck on the pommel of the saddle. He sat without moving anything except the hand holding the cigarette, until he had smoked it down to a small butt. He exhaled the last lungful of the acrid smoke and ground out the butt on the heel of his boot.

'I 'spect that's a habit I'll soon be shucking,' he muttered, remembering Katy's distaste for the smell of tobacco on his breath.

It would be a trade he'd gladly make. He hadn't smoked very much before the war. Not at all when he and Katy had fallen in love. But, he convinced himself, he needed the calming effect of the nicotine in the war.

That conviction had almost cost him his life twice. Behind Confederate lines, scouting for information, it had been the smoke of his cigarette that had betrayed his presence to an alert Confederate States Army sentry. Either time, if he had been a split-second slower, or a trace less accurate with the Navy Colt he had then worn on his hip, he would have been dead. As it was, it was the Southern sentries who died, and he who was fleeing for his life, until he had reached his own unit.

He shook his head, shedding the host of unwelcome memories. He willed himself to replace them with prior and much more pleasant memories. His eyes slid, as if on cue, to the blackberry bushes along the bank of Cold Creek. He could almost see the berry buckets he and Katy had carried. His eyes were drawn as if by a magnet to the place they had set them down, when he grabbed her and pretended he was going to throw her into the creek. He still knew that exact spot. It was the first time he had dared to kiss her. She had squealed and wrapped her arms around his neck to keep from being thrown in the ice-cold water. It was as if she were reading his mind, knowing precisely what he was hoping she would do. She turned her face toward him, their lips inches apart. It seemed the most natural thing in the world that the space between those two pairs of lips should disappear.

He could taste her lips in his mind, even now. He could feel the shape of her body pressed against him, as a rising tide of desire had threatened to dissolve all restraint between them. He still wondered how far she would have gone if he had pressed the moment.

He hadn't. He still wasn't sure whether to be proud of his restraint, or to regret passing up the opportunity. When she pulled back, cheeks rosy with a mixture of embarrassment and desire, he let her do so. Awkwardness sprang up between them for just a moment, and he feared she would run away.

Instead her eyes began to dance. Dimples appeared magically at the corners of her mouth. She said, 'I'd begun to think you were never going to get around to that, Marion Denning.'

Instantly the awkwardness dissipated. He grinned. 'If you aren't careful, I'll do it again, Katy Dowling.'

'Well! I certainly hope so!' she quipped. She picked up her berry bucket and walked away toward a bush laden with the dark berries, her hips swaying provocatively.

Abruptly the pleasant memory snapped from his mind. His horse's ears abruptly went forward, his head turning slightly to the left.

Red's foot uncurled from around the saddle horn and returned to the stirrup. His hand dropped to his gun butt, even as his head swiveled to identify the source of his horse's attention.

A rider emerged from a copse of aspen, a hundred yards to his left. Red relaxed almost at once. A faint smile played at the corners of his mouth.

The rider approached at a swift trot, hauling his horse to a stop a dozen feet in front of Red. He spit a brown streak of tobacco juice at the top of a clump of scrub sage. He wiped his mouth with the back of his hand, then spoke. 'I heard there was apt t' be strange drifters wanderin' through, now that the fightin's over.'

Red pulled the fixings from his shirt

pocket and began to roll a smoke. 'The strangest ones stayed where they could see the mountains, just in case they needed to hightail it over 'em.'

The newcomer spit again. 'Thet was the smart ones.'

He nudged his horse closer, reaching out a thickly calloused hand. 'How are ya, Red?'

Red took the hand and returned its iron grip. He marveled at the way the feel of that handshake radiated a sense of well-being clear through him. 'Still keepin' body 'n soul together, Hank.'

'That's been no small task, I'm bettin'.'

'There were times it wasn't a safe bet, that's for sure.'

'I'm sure thet's a fact. When did ya git back?'

'Just now gettin' here. Ain't even been down to the house yet.'

'She's a wee bit worse fer wear.'

'Bound to be. Still fixable?'

'Oh, sure. You bilt 'er solid. What's it been, two years? Two an' a half? Couple o' them fancy glass winders ya stuck in it is busted out. Shales blowed off the roof here'n there. Nothin' ya can't git whipped inta shape in a couple o' weeks, the way ya tear into stuff.'

Red's eyes twinkled. 'Well, if the neighbors were more help, I wouldn't have to work so hard.'

Hank Wistrom's expression didn't change. 'If'n ya had any decent neighbors, I 'spect they would.'

Red chuckled. 'Doesn't hurt to hope they been gettin' better while I've been gone.'

'Still ridin' thet jug-headed bay, I see.'

Red nodded. 'He made it through the whole war, Hank. Saved my bacon more'n once.'

'Good horse'll do thet fer ya, all right.'

'Your herd doin' OK?'

Hank nodded. 'Right good. Been mild the last couple winters. Calving went good. Can't complain. My herd's built up some better'n yours, I 'spect.'

Red's expression sobered perceptibly.

'Mine aren't doing so well?'

Hank studied his face a long moment before he replied. 'They ain't done as bad's they mighta, jist left runnin' wild thataway, whilst ya went trottin' off t' war an' all,' he hedged. 'There was plenty o' feed fer 'em t' rustle through the winters. Thet ain't been no problem. I have noticed a few o' your cows with Rafter K calves a-suckin', though.'

Red's lips tightened. 'Kaiser's boys been a little long with their ropes, have they?'

'Well, now, I wouldn't be the one t' say they was long-ropin' or nothin'. Jist thought it a mite strange how calves with their brand was a suckin' cows what had your Flyin' O on 'em. Jist thought maybe Kaiser'd hired some o' your,' cows t' wet-nurse his orphaned calves er somethin'.'

'I may have a talk with Groon.'

'Ya might wanta do that, right enough. Not jist 'bout bein' careless what calves he's been a-tryin' t' stick 'is brand on, though.'

Red's eyebrows rose. 'That so? What else?'

Hank spit again, once more wiping his

mouth with the back of his hand. 'Don't wanta start nothin', like some gossipy ol' woman, or thet,' he evaded. 'Ya jist might wanta pay some special attention to what's important to ya, though.'

'Meaning Katy?'

Hank's eyes flashed briefly. 'I didn't say that. Now that ya mention it, though, there's been some lot o' talk 'bout him pushin' purty hard in that direction. Seems to've made hisself her ol' man's best friend, 'e has. Matter o' fact, Pat Dowling's herd's grown' faster'n anybody's in the valley. His buildin's is sure in fine shape, too. Some o' Kaiser's boys been seen over there helpin' out, time t' time. If'n I was one t' gossip, I'd likely be talkin' 'bout how heavy Kaiser's a-shinin' up t' that little ol' girl, all right.'

Red nodded. 'We've been writing real steady the whole time I been gone. She told me he's been trying plumb hard to convince her I'm not coming back.'

'He ain't gonna be pleased none t' see ya are back.'

'I'll see if I can't make him real unhappy.'

Hank grinned, showing scraggly, tobacco-browned teeth. 'Let me know when'n where. That there's a meetin' I'll be wantin' a good front seat at.'

'So how's your family?' Red asked.

Hank nodded his head. 'Finer'n frogs' hair. Ma, she's put on a little weight. Jimmy's pertneart ten now. Allie's six, an' sassier'n a brooder hen.'

'That's good to hear. Tell 'em hi for me.'

'I'll do that fer sure. Ma'll be plumb tickled you're back in the country. Why don't ya come on over fer supper tomorrer?'

'How about the day after?' Red countered. 'I'm hopin' Katy's mom'll ask me to stay for supper tomorrow.'

'Ya waitin' till tomorrer t' even go see 'er? What'sa matter with ya, boy? Ya wantin' 'er t' think ya ain't anxious t' see 'er?'

Red grinned. 'She knows better'n that. I sure don't want to show up looking like I've been two weeks in the saddle the first time she sees me.'

'Ya have been two weeks in the saddle, I'm bettin'.'

'All o' that. Good night's sleep, a bath, some clean clothes, and I'll look a bit better to her.'

Hank spit again, followed by the inevitable swipe of his hand across his mouth. 'Took my bath last month, a'ready. Figgered t' wait closer t' hot weather, but Ma was gettin' a mite testy.'

'Women do have a way of wanting their man to smell good.'

Hank snorted his agreement. 'I figger if'n the smell don't bother me, it shouldn't bother her. Ain't figgered out how come she don't think so. She makes them poor kids take a bath every single week, she does, winter'n summer. Wonder they don't catch their death. If'n I was a mite less stubborn she'd likely have me doin' the same.'

Red's mouth twisted in an effort to keep a straight face. 'I sure wouldn't want to see anything like that happen to you, Hank.'

'I gotta git goin',' Hank offered, instead of

answering. His eyes grew serious as he studied Red's face. 'They's some hard-lookin' fellers workin' fer Kaiser, these days. Might have t' do with rumors ya was on yer way back. Ya watch yer back, Red.'

'I'm kind of in the habit of doin' that,' Red responded. 'Tell Dottie and the kids hi for me,' he said again.

Without responding Hank lifted a hand as he wheeled his horse and rode away at a swift trot. Red sat watching his friend ride away until he disappeared over a low rise. He sighed heavily. He ground out the butt of his cigarette carefully on the pommel of his saddle, and spoke to his horse. 'Well, Useless, it looks like we got our work cut out for us.'

The conviction settled uncomfortably on him that he had only heard the first whispers of what lay ahead.

CHAPTER 3

'Still wearin' them shiny Union boots, huh?'

Red immediately identified the source of the implied challenge. His hand brushed the butt of his Russian .44.

A nondescript cowboy leaned against the front wall of The Waterhole Saloon, one of two the thriving town of Lennox boasted. The pointed toes of his boots were curled up slightly, worn almost through. The bottom of his pants' legs, pulled over the top of his boots, were tattered and ragged. His shirt was threadbare. A leather vest was his only item of clothing that looked to be in good repair. His hat brim drooped down around his face as though too weak to support its own weight.

He was as thin as a scraggly fence post. He had not shaved for a week or so. His face seemed to have long since forgotten the feel of a smile. A holster of scratched-up leather on his hip held a Colt .45.

'Were you speaking to me?' Red enquired. He stopped his course down the street and took several steps toward the cowboy.

'I don't see nobody else wanderin' down the street,' the cowboy observed. 'Jist back from the war, huh?'

Red nodded. 'Just back, and sure hoping it's over and done.'

The cowboy reached into his shirt pocket for his fixings. He glared at Red in silence as he tore a cigarette paper off the packet. He shaped it into a trough, then carefully sprinkled tobacco into it from the bag of Bull Durham. In spite of the evident liquor on his breath, he held the paper trough of tobacco steady as he gripped the tag in his teeth and pulled the drawstring shut. He replaced the bag of tobacco in his shirt pocket. Using both hands he rolled the paper around the tobacco. He ran his tongue along the edge of the paper, using the moisture to seal the tobacco-filled tube. He twisted one end of the paper, and put the other end into his mouth.

He reached into his shirt pocket again and pulled out a wooden match. He lifted one foot, to tighten the trouser material along the back of his leg. He whipped the match head along the tightly stretched pants' leg. It emitted a wisp of smoke and burst into flame. He touched the match to the twisted end of the cigarette and inhaled. The cigarette flared, then glowed softly.

He shook the fire from the match and tossed it into the street. He inhaled deeply, and blew out a great cloud of smoke. All the while he made no effort to speak. His eyes bored holes into Red. Red started to speak several times, but then held his peace and waited.

Finally the cowboy said, 'Things ain't never gonna be the same, are they?'

'No, I don't suppose they will. It'll fade though, if we let it.'

'If there was a God, He'da stopped it.'

'You don't think there is one?'

The cowboy took another long drag on his cigarette. He exhaled slowly, looking into the cloud of smoke as into a mirror of the past. When he spoke again his voice was softer, more distant.

'I used to s'pose there was,' he said finally. 'Not no more.'

Red studied the cowboy. His face was the color of old leather, wrinkled as the skin of a raisin. That, too, could have been from age or from too many years' exposure to the harsh sun and weather of Wyoming. He could have been anywhere from forty to eighty years old, he decided.

'What's your name?'

'Josh Biddle. Yers?'

'Red Denning.'

'You the one homesteaded out on Cold Crick?'

'That's me.'

'I ride fer Kaiser.'

'When did you stop believing in God?' Red asked abruptly, relaxing his hand, letting it drift away from his gun butt.

Josh took another long drag. He dropped the remains of his cigarette. He ground it out with the worn sole of his boot. He again studied the cloud of smoke as he exhaled. When he looked back at Red his eyes glinted with hard bitterness.

Josh ignored the question for the moment. 'Who'd ya ride with?'

'Gregg.'

Josh nodded. 'I was with the Tennessee Volunteers. Fought under Bragg, may his rotten soul burn in Hell.'

Red couldn't resist the first thought that struck his mind. 'What makes you think there's a Hell? If you don't believe in God, why would you believe in Hell?'

The irony didn't faze the man. ''Cause I know Hell is real. I been there. I been through Hell. All the way through.'

Red held his silence, waiting for the troubled cowboy to continue.

After a long pause, he did. 'Let me tell you what the war was like, from our side,

Yankee. It started off like some great romantic notion o' bein' a patriotic hero. We was all gonna march off in our fancy gray uniforms, and shoot us a whole slew o' you Yankees, and then come marchin' home a' singin' victory songs. Then we was a-gonna thank God fer makin' us heroes.'

He stopped and dug out the makings again. He fashioned another cigarette and lit it, throwing the match down. Once again he studied the smoke in silence. When he spoke, his voice was back to that softer, more distant tone again.

'But it wasn't like that. It didn't take long for the purty gray uniform to get dirty and tattered and ugly. Bloody too, time after time, plumb to the knees, sometimes, an' none of it mine. Our shoes wore out, an' they warn't no fancy boots like them o' yours to take their place. We run outa food. We ate sparrows an' rats an' our own horses an' mules, sometimes. We boiled leaves an' bark an' ate it till we got sick. An' we all knowed we was in the right, an' God would give us the victory, sooner or later, 'cause we was good Christian boys, an' we was fightin' fer the right. An' we kept a-havin' at you Yankees, what thought God was a-fightin' on your side, just like we thought He was fightin' on ours.'

Red didn't attempt to answer. He leaned back against a post that supported a roof over the sidewalk, and waited in attentive silence. After another long drag, Josh continued, 'It were sich a long war. I 'spect it was jist as long fer y'all. It went on fer months an' months an' months. We lost track o' time, 'cept by when we was sweatin' fit to die, an' when we was freezin' to death. An' whenever the big shots like Bragg figured we oughta, we'd set to with you Yankees agin. You'd have at us with yer canister an' cannon, an' we'd have at y'all the same. Then someone'd decide it was time t' kill each other up close some more, an' we'd go chargin' at each other. Then afore we knowed it, we'd be standin' there knee deep in blood, with dead an' dyin' men all around us, jist tryin' t' survive.'

He stopped to take another drag of his

cigarette. Red watched the same scenes parade across his own mind as he kept silence, letting the other man talk.

He did. 'Me'n Clay Whitcomb was together, when we went in. We was real lucky, till we got up by Murphysboro. We was hunkered down together behind this big ol' tree the wind had blowed over. We was shootin' over the top of it, an' a-rackin' up a purty good score on you Yankees. Then Clay turns to me an' was jist a-fixin' to say somethin' when a ball went right through his head, side t' side. His eyes jist sorta went flat, an' he didn't never get to finish what he was sayin'. He jist sorta fell over, an' I knowed he was dead. I still wonder, sometimes, what he was goin' to tell me.'

He stared into space for several minutes again, before he continued. 'I hope it wasn't nothin' important, what he was fixin' to say. Thet thar was the most God-awful battle we had the whole war. We fought an' run an' fought an' run. We prayed, too. We prayed an' begged an' pleaded with God to do somethin'. Anythin'. But He didn't. He didn't do nothin'. It jist went on an' on an' on.'

He took another puff of his cigarette. 'We didn't stop prayin', though. We prayed pert-neart as hard as we fought. We figgered He was God, so He must know what He was doin'.'

In the wafting clouds of his smoke he studied the images that only he could see, that he could not stop seeing. When he spoke again, his voice was tired and old.

'Somewheres along there, I figured out there jist warn't no God after all. If there was, they ain't no way He coulda stood it to watch all that killin' an' screamin' an' Him doin' nothin' to put a stop to it. I jist decided I warn't gonna never believe in Him no more.'

Red spoke finally. His voice was soft, swollen with his own memories and surging emotions. 'That doesn't make it any easier to live with, though, does it?'

Josh looked directly at him again. He laughed shortly. ''Course not. It's jist kept on bein' hell ever since. I 'spect it always will, too, but that's the way it is.'

'It'll fade with time, if we let it,' Red said, knowing he was repeating himself. Josh's voice grew more distant. 'Why didn't He jist reach down and say, "Thet's enough", and haul it up short? Why did He jist let it go on an' on, till they warn't hardly a man left alive that was a whole man no more?'

Instead of answering, Red said, 'Can I buy you a drink?'

Josh looked at him as if seeing him for the first time. 'Ya'd buy a busted down ol' Johnny Reb a drink?'

'And proud to, Josh Biddle.'

Josh studied him a long moment. He shrugged his bony shoulders and slouched upright from the wall that was supporting him. 'Why not?'

As Red tossed his money on the bar and they gave their orders to the bartender, he thought, well, maybe there's at least one that I won't have to kill.

CHAPTER 4

Pat Dowling sure knew a fine spot to locate a ranch yard. Every time Red topped this rise, he stopped and admired the perfection of the location. The buildings were on a low hill, shadowed on the south and west by higher hills, forested with tall timber, sheltering the ranch buildings from most winter storms. The view, especially toward the east, was clear and unobstructed. The house was located to maximize the enjoyment of that view.

The house was log, with a covered porch across the entire front. From that porch, or through the large windows behind it, the country unfolded in layers of beauty as it descended toward the Wind River in the distance.

To the north the ground fell away toward

Beaver Creek, babbling its hurried path over multicolored rocks that sought to prevent its merge with Cold Creek.

Timber extending south and west, up the mountains, was a mixture of pine, spruce and cedar, with clumps of aspen mingled in occasionally. The aspen were more in evidence along the creek, where they brushed branches with giant cottonwoods. Brush grew heavily along the creek, as it did in the bottoms of all the draws that extended outward from it.

On the large knoll that hosted the house, the barn, bunkhouse and the corrals were organized carefully to facilitate ranch operation to the fullest.

Red frowned as he surveyed the yard and buildings. The porch of the house, the bunkhouse, even the barn sported fresh red paint. It was rare to see buildings painted in that country, let alone as glaringly as the Dowling ranch.

The entrance to the yard was flanked by a tall pole at each side of the road. They supported a long board, with large printing done with the same bright red paint. 'Dowling Land and Cattle Company,' boasted one line, with 'Patrick Dowling, Proprietor,' on the line beneath. At either end of the lettering, the Double-D-Bar brand bracketed the boast.

Several thoughts flitted across Red's mind at the pretentious efforts to exude prosperity. He quickly brushed them aside. After all, Dowling was Katy's father. Red ought not allow himself to harbor an unnecessarily derogatory attitude.

He considered riding around the ostentatious sign rather than beneath it, but then shrugged and nudged Useless forward. Just as he did, a furry blur separated from the far side of the ranch house, streaking toward him. Grinning, Red leaped from the saddle and dropped to one knee. 'Hey, Pal!' he called.

The nondescript black and white dog covered the distance between them with amazing speed, sliding to a halt against the master he had despaired of seeing again. Left with the Dowlings when Red went off to war, he had stationed himself at the yard gate for nearly a year, refusing to leave his post except to eat and drink. Winter and summer he slept there, watching, waiting for his owner to return. Only in the last months had he abandoned that vigil, and even then kept watch from the porch of the house most days.

He whined and whimpered softly as Red took his head in both hands, ruffling his fur, rubbing his ears, talking softly to him. When he released him, the dog danced in circles around him, panting happily. Soft sounds between a whine and a growl issued from his throat.

Red grinned and reached down to pet the animal again, then straightened and stepped back into the saddle. As he did, he said, 'Heel, Pal.'

Instantly, as if no time had elapsed, the dog took his position just behind and to the left of Red's mount, keeping the exact distance as the horse trotted forward.

As they approached the house, a man walked swiftly across the yard toward him. Pat Dowling's slight body was dwarfed by an obviously new, spotlessly white hat. Its tall crown and broad brim made his rubicund face seem even smaller and redder than usual. Tufts of orange-red hair poked from beneath the sweatband, blending with the beard that was restricted to his jaw-line and chin.

'Well, so 'tis comin' back ye are after all,' he said as he drew closer.

Red's jaw tightened despite his efforts to smile. Most folks ask you to get down and come in, he thought.

Instead of voicing his notice of the obvious lack of a courteous greeting, he swung un-asked from the saddle. He extended a hand to the rancher, noticing the signs of ageing around his face. Gray was crowding its way into the red of his whiskers with surprising vigor. 'You're looking good, Pat,' he offered.

Pat Dowling's eyes bored into him as he took the hand, gripping it firmly after only a moment's hesitation. ''Tis good I'm doin', it is. And bein' a bit surprised at ye comin' back from sich a war lookin' all fit an' nary a scratch upon ye.'

'I was lucky,' Red responded.

'Got t' be more'n luck, I'm thinkin',' Pat protested. ''Tis good ye must've got at stayin' where the dyin' was less.'

Ignoring the implication, Red said, 'Your place is looking awfully fine.'

Pat looked around at his bright red buildings with obvious pride. ''Tis mighty fine that a little paint makes a place, don't ye agree, now?'

With a perfectly straight face Red said, 'It sure makes the place stand out. Do you plan to paint the corral fences too?'

Pat's eyebrows rose slightly. He studied Red's face, as if to ascertain whether he was being serious or mocking him. Deciding the question was serious, he turned back and studied the corrals. 'Well, now, I hadn't been givin' that a thought, but it might not be a bad thing. 'Twas Groon's idea to be paintin' the buildin's. Says it preserves the wood a good bit longer'n it'd last without it.'

Red's lips compressed at the mention of Kaiser's name, but he said nothing. Instead he offered, 'Must've taken a lot of time and work to get it all put on.'

'Sure an' it was for a fact,' Pat agreed, 'but worth every bit of it. Th'ain't a place in the country can be lookin' finer, I'm thinkin'.'

'It does make the place look prosperous,' Red hedged.

'Well, now ye be comin' in,' Pat said, belatedly conceding to common courtesy. 'Ye'll be stayin' for dinner, an' supper too, I'm guessin'.'

It sounded more like something the rancher was resigned to than inviting, but Red merely said, 'Thanks. I'd like that. It's been a long time since I've filled up on Cally's fine cooking.'

Pat snorted. ''Tis not the cookin' ye'r comin' 'round for, an' there's no denyin' that.'

Red grinned. 'Well, I do like the cooking too.'

Pat started to answer, but was interrupted by a squeal from the porch. Cally Dowling flew down the steps, the lightness of her actions belying her ample figure. She ran toward Red, arms outstretched. 'You're back, Red! Katy told me you'd be here any day! Oh, Red, it's so good to see you.'

She grabbed him in a great hug that he returned with equal enthusiasm. She stepped back, but kept her hands at his waist. She looked him up and down as if preparing to bid on him at auction. 'Oh my, Red, you look good! I was so afraid you'd be killed, or come home with an arm or a leg gone, like so many have done. Oh, Katy will be so happy to see you.'

Muttering something unintelligible, Pat stalked off toward the barn. Cally ignored him completely. After he was out of earshot, she said, 'Doesn't this place look absolutely hideous? Can you believe this? Bright red! Makes the place look like a big whorehouse, and you don't have to excuse me for saying the word. He could at least have painted my porch white, if he was determined to paint it, but no! Groon says red paint is the best. Groon says it lasts longer. Groon says it weathers better. Groon says this. Groon says that. I swear that man of mine doesn't even have a mind of his own anymore.'

'It does show up from a ways off,' Red offered.

Cally snorted her displeasure. 'Shows up like a sunbonnet on a sow hog!'

'It will make the rain run off better, I 'spect,' he grinned.

She snorted again, and backed away from him. 'Katy's down along the crick, gatherin' greens. You can put your horse up and trot on down there. She just might be a little bit happy to see you.'

'She better be,' he replied, as much to himself as to Cally.

Pat was nowhere in sight when he put his horse away. He measured out some oats into his feed box and tossed a fork of hay into the manger. He fished a whole clove out of the shirt pocket where he used to carry his makings. He put it in his mouth to sweeten his breath, then headed toward the creek at a fast walk.

The closer to the creek he got, the faster he walked. His eyes scanned up and down the stream for any sign of her. In minutes he spotted grass that was bent, a small twig that had been kicked, so the moist side was upward, a dozen small signs only the eye of an expert tracker would spot. Without even thinking about it, his eye followed the faint trail. His mind calculated the time since she had passed. His ears tensed for any sound of her movement.

It took him less than fifteen minutes to catch up to her. She was in a clearing, scanning the tall, lush grass for the greens she sought. Her back was toward him.

Red stopped in his tracks when he saw her. His chest constricted suddenly. He felt as out of breath as if he'd just run a mile. His heart hammered. He forced himself to take a deep breath, his eyes never leaving the young woman. He made himself move slowly, silently. He walked to a tree at the edge of the clearing. He pulled a long blade of grass, sticking one end of it in his mouth. He leaned against the tree, crossing his legs, striking an exaggerated pose of nonchalance.

He spoke quietly, but she jumped as if she'd been shot at the sound of his voice. 'Are you looking for something in particular?'

She whirled, dropping the basket that was half filled with greens. A squeal that sounded eerily like her mother's left her mouth. 'Red! Oh, Red,' she cried.

She gathered her skirts and lifted them, heading toward him as fast as she could run. His exaggerated nonchalance dissipated quicker than fog in a desert wind. He ran to meet her, catching her up in his arms and whirling her around, before pulling her to himself.

Her arms wrapped around him. She buried her face in his chest, pressing her body against him. He bent his head down, letting the feel of her body, the scent of her hair, the pounding of her heart melt away two years of loneliness. Neither moved for several minutes, as if willing the moment to last forever.

Finally she relaxed the grip of her arms. He responded by doing the same. She moved back just enough to tip her head back and look up into his eyes. Their lips met as if it were the most natural move either of them could imagine.

They separated, looked wordlessly into each other's eyes, then moved together again in a longer, deeper kiss. Her tongue darted between his lips teasingly for just an instant. His own tongue followed hers back into her mouth, where her tongue welcomed it in a glad dance of reunion. When she pulled away, Red resisted the urge to jerk her back to himself. She stepped back as his fingers trailed along her arms and fell away. 'Oh, Red,' she said. Her voice was husky. 'I have waited and prayed and longed for this moment for so very, very long. I was so afraid you wouldn't come back to me.'

'It'd take more than a few Johnny Rebs to

keep me away from you.'

A shadow crossed her eyes. Her brow pulled down into a furrowed 'V' between her deep-blue eyes. 'No it wouldn't, Marion Denning,' she protested. 'It would only take one stray bullet, one piece of shrapnel, one cannon ball to take you away from me forever. I have lived with that danger for almost two years. Don't just brush it off like you were never in danger.'

His own eyes darkened as he drew her to himself, wrapping his arms around her again. 'It doesn't do any good to dwell on it. Anyway, it didn't happen. I'm home. To stay.'

She pulled back, looking up into his eyes. 'You resigned your commission?'

'You bet. That's what took me so long getting home to you. I wanted it all done, so I wouldn't have to worry about having to leave you again.'

Relief washed through her eyes. Her chin came up. Her voice took on a saucy tone. 'Sit down here and tell me how happy you are to see me, Marion Denning.'

She dropped to her knees, then sat back, with her legs doubled back beside her. She spread her skirt out on the deep grass, covering her feet. Its pattern framed the perfect beauty of her form, her face, with its bridge of freckles across her nose, the reddish-brown hair that cascaded down across her shoulders in loose curls.

The catch in his throat threatened his ability to breathe. He sat down beside her, his hand extended back and to the side supporting him. His voice was soft, fraught with emotion. 'I don't have the words to tell you that.'

'You could give it a try.'

He reached out and put an arm around her, pulling her to himself as he lay down on the deep, soft carpet of grass. She responded willingly, lying down on her side, facing him. He kissed her again, savoring the feel, the taste of her full lips and their responsiveness. Their tongues met again, curling around each other, each tasting the flavor hidden deep beneath the other's. 'Cloves,' she said softly, between kisses. 'I love cloves. Especially on your tongue.'

Time and space lost all meaning to him, and there was suddenly nothing in the world except him and her, and the boundless love he felt for her.

The distant clanging of a dinner bell intruded rudely into the moment. She pulled back from him, an impish smile playing at the corners of her mouth. 'Why, Marion Denning, I do believe you're trying to take advantage of me.'

A momentary surge of disappointment was quickly eclipsed by the joy of her presence. He smiled in return. 'You'd better be careful, Katy Dowling, because that's exactly what I intend to do.'

She stood, brushing imaginary dust or grass from her skirt. 'All in good time, my darling,' she said. 'Just be sure you make an honest woman of me first.'

'Just say the word.'

'I can't.'

'You can't? Why not?'

'Because you haven't asked me yet. Isn't it proper for a man to ask for a woman's hand, before they begin planning such things?'

He grasped both of her hands, dropped to one knee, and spoke in an exaggerated Southern drawl. 'Miss Dowling, would y'all do me the honor of becoming Mrs Denning?'

She giggled, then responded in the same drawl. 'Why, Mr Denning, this is so sudden! I never imagined y'all had such designs on little ol' me!'

The drawl disappeared from his voice. 'Do you always lie like that?'

She giggled again. 'Do you want me to?'

'To what?'

'Lie.'

'Of course not. I want you to say you'll be my wife.'

'OK. You'll be my wife.'

Laughter exploded from him. 'Let's try that again. I want you to say I'll be your wife.'

She opened her mouth to ask how he planned to be her wife, but the deep seriousness in his eyes stopped her. Instead she said,

'I would be the happiest woman in the world to be your wife, Marion Denning.'

The dancing light came back into his eyes. 'I believe that's a yes.'

'You'd better believe that's a yes,' she confirmed, as he stood and took her in his arms again.

Neither of them ever remembered what they ate, when they responded to that insistent, intruding dinner bell.

CHAPTER 5

The dog growled softly. Instantly Red's eyes darted to the dog, then away in the direction the animal was studying. He could see nothing.

'What do you hear, Pal?' he asked softly.

He wiped the sweat from his hands. His right hand brushed the walnut grips of his Russian .44, reassuring himself it was ready for instant use.

He glanced around. Two weeks of back-breaking work had erased most signs of desertion from the well-built structure. The broken windows were not yet replaced, but he had ordered them from the General Store in Lennox. They should arrive within the next three weeks.

The roof was repaired. The door once again swung easily and silently. The small animals that had taken up residence in his absence had been evicted. The interior was scrubbed spotless and smelled of lye soap. It was nearly ready. He would be proud to bring his bride home to this place in just over a month.

With obvious reluctance, Katy's father had agreed to the date. Word had been sent to the circuit riding parson, and his presence was assured. Katy and her mother were busy as a pair of beavers sewing, planning, chattering and celebrating. In what started as a life threatening challenge, he had befriended the Confederate veteran,

Josh Biddle. It was incredible that he had made a friend of the staunchest Rebel in the valley. He and Hank Wistrom had both dropped in to help with the work on the house, from time to time.

Fewer than he had expected of his cattle were missing. He had spotted his beloved team of mules, and planned to catch them later in the day. Life was good.

He swung his gaze again to where the dog still watched intently, whining softly every few seconds. From over the ridge, a covey of sage hens erupted into the air. 'Sure enough someone's coming,' he told his dog quietly.

In less than a minute the heads of two riders appeared, riding at a swift trot. As they approached, Red's jaw tightened. His hand brushed the butt of his pistol again. 'Watch my back, Pal,' he muttered.

The dog gave no indication of response, but Red knew the dog would warn him of anyone else's approach. He could give his whole attention to the certain trouble that was rapidly approaching.

Groon Kaiser continued without slowing until he was closer than either Red or Pal was comfortable with. The dog growled a snarled warning, baring his teeth threateningly. The horse responded before Kaiser did, skidding to a halt, prancing nervously, edging back away from the snarling menace. Kaiser cursed, lashing the horse's rump with the quirt that hung from a strap from his left wrist. The mount squealed and reared slightly, but refused to crowd closer to man and dog.

Kaiser's face reddened. He lifted the quirt to whip the animal more severely. At the last moment he lowered the whip, jerking painfully on the reins instead.

The second man had reined in quicker than Kaiser. He turned his horse slightly, positioning himself for swift access to his holstered gun. Without seeming to, Red assessed the man carefully.

He was thin and wiry, of about average height. His clothes were too good, and too clean, to identify him as a working cowboy.

The well-used gun on his hip added to the clear picture of a hired gunman.

The gunman's face was thin and pointed, with a long nose that seemed to extend just a bit too far forward. His black eyes were small and close-set. Dark hair was slicked back beneath a low, flat-crowned hat. All in all he presented an image that brought one word to Red's mind. Weasel, he thought silently.

'Morning, Groon,' Red said, his voice deceptively soft.

Kaiser took another couple minutes to fight his horse under control. Unable to use the animal to crowd Red backward, he let it suffice to curse the hapless animal instead. Finally he addressed Red. 'I heard you were back.'

'I'm back,' Red responded.

'Lot's o' men didn't make it back.'

'Good lot of 'em died.'

'Too bad you weren't among 'em.'

'I'm just as happy to see you, too,' Red smiled mirthlessly.

'You probably killed some good men to be

able to make it back.'

'Every Johnny Reb I had to kill was a better man than you'll ever be.'

Kaiser's hand dropped to the butt of his gun, but he swiftly abandoned that idea.

Red's stance allowed no mistake about his readiness to accept a challenge.

'Maybe you'd oughta introduce us,' the weasel spoke for the first time. 'Might be this fella hasn't recognized me.'

Kaiser's eyes darted from Red to the gunman and back again. 'This here's Billy Hand,' he offered.

Red's eyes never left the gunman, nor bore any expression. 'Is that name supposed to mean something to me?'

'It should,' Hand replied. 'Most folks have heard of me. I've probably killed more men up close than you managed to kill from a distance in the war.'

'Is that so?' Red responded. 'Were any of them facing you at the time?'

The gunman's eyes flashed fire, but the faint smile never left his lips. His voice was soft. 'If you don't think so, you might want to go for your own gun.'

Before Red could respond, Kaiser said, 'I didn't ride clear over here to pick a fight with you, Denning.'

Red's gaze stayed fixed on the gunman, watching Kaiser only from the corner of his eye. 'Then spit out what you want and get off my place. You're not welcome here.'

'I came to give you a fair chance to ride out of this country while you can.'

'Are you threatening me, Kaiser?'

'I'm telling you. There's talk around about things you was doin' in the war. You ain't likely to be welcome in this valley.'

'Talk? What talk would that be, if you don't mind my asking?'

'Just talk. Seems maybe you wasn't what you pretended to be durin' the war.'

Confusion and anger mingled together in Red's mind, tumbling over each other. For the first time he could remember he felt hesitant, uncertain.

'I have no idea what you're talking about.'

'I'm guessin' ya do. Anyway, you'd just as well ride on anyway. There's nothin' in this valley for you to stay around for.'

'Well, you're dead wrong there, Kaiser. I got the best reason in the world to stay in this valley for the rest of my life.'

Kaiser's face reddened again. 'That there's what I wanted to let ya know, Denning. Just so there ain't no mistakes. I been courtin' your girl ... the one that *was* your girl ... I been courtin' Katy Dowling since ya been gone off t' war. I intend to marry her, Denning. You're out of the picture. Stay away from her.'

Red laughed harshly. 'Would you listen to that? You're dumber than I thought you were, Kaiser. Katy can't stand you, and wouldn't marry you if she had to live out her life as an old maid instead. Besides, you don't think I'd have been back this long without seeing her, do you?'

'Stay away from her,' Kaiser gritted.

Red laughed again. 'Not a chance, Kaiser. The lady has agreed to marry me, and we've set the date for the wedding. Just over a month away, as a matter of fact. I guess you're about the only one in the valley that's not invited.'

Kaiser's mouth opened and closed several times before he spoke. He looked comically like a fish at the edge of a fish bowl, opening and closing its mouth. Finally he said, 'You're lyin', Denning. Her pa would never allow her to marry the likes of you. We got an understanding.'

'You're wrong again, Kaiser. He gave us his blessing.'

Kaiser sputtered, 'He wouldn't do that. Not after all I've done for him. Not after the way I've built up his herd.'

Red cut in. 'Yeah, I heard you've been tryin' real hard to buy him. Whatever else he is, Pat Dowling isn't for sale, Kaiser. Especially not for a few buckets of ugly red paint from an uglier bag of hot air.'

Kaiser pointed a dirty finger at Red, stabbing the air for emphasis as he spoke. 'You will not live to marry that woman if you try to stay in this valley! She is mine! You have nothing. You are nothing.'

'I got a right nice place here,' Red argued. 'At least it suits Katy. My cows are doing fine. And, oh, by the way, I've been riding around checking on how my cattle did while I was gone. They look real good, except there's an awful lot of them that have calves sucking that seem to have your brand on them. I took the trouble to ride over to Rimrock, and had the sheriff ride out with me to have a look. He saw twenty-five or thirty like that, right off, without looking hard. I'm sure you wouldn't condone any long-roping, but it seems maybe your hands got a little careless about which calves they were slapping your brand on. What I wondered was whether you intended to pay me for all those calves that have your brand on them, or just give me a bill of sale for them, so there won't be any question about their being mine.'

News that the sheriff had documented Flying O cows nursing Rafter K calves visibly unsettled Kaiser. Even he was not immune from the country's decisive and deadly hatred of rustlers. If he defended the branding of Red's calves, he would be classed as such immediately. If he didn't, he'd either have to pay for the calves or give Red clear title to them. Either way was backing down, and Grunwald Kaiser had never backed down from anyone in his life.

Kaiser's fingers curled and flexed. His eyes jumped back and forth from Red to the gunfighter at his side. It was clear he wanted more than anything in the world to draw his gun and kill Red on the spot. Even through his hot rage, however, a small voice of reason reminded him that Red was amazingly swift and accurate with a six-shooter. He knew he didn't stand a chance against him. It was just as clear that he wasn't sure he and Hand together would fare any better.

Instead he said, 'It will not matter, Denning. I'll have you out of this country or dead, long before the day you think you're marrying my girl.'

'She ain't your girl, Kaiser. Never was.

Never will be.'

'We will see about that. We will see how well the people in this valley will allow a man like you to live among them.'

With that he wheeled his horse and galloped from the yard, sitting flat in the saddle. The gunman remained as he was, his eyes locked with Red's. Finally he said, 'You'd best remember the name of Billy Hand, Denning. Ask around. You might have better sense than to try to stand up to me again.'

He broke off the gaze and turned his horse, galloping after his boss. Watching them out of sight, Red muttered, 'Kaiser still rides like a sack of potatoes tied in the saddle.'

He stood there for several minutes, puzzling over Kaiser's threats. What could there possibly be from his military record that would create any kind of problem? Would the rancher stoop to planting totally false rumors, to turn people against him? Wouldn't they be easy to refute if he did? Why did he seem so confident, in the face of obvious defeat with Katy?

Finally he shrugged, and turned toward the barn. 'Let's saddle up a horse and see if we can catch those mules, Pal.'

CHAPTER 6

'Well, Useless, there they are. Most of 'em, anyway. Do you think us an' Pal can get 'em back and in the corral?'

Red sat his horse on a low rise, surveying a grassy expanse before him. In the background, and ranging out to both sides, cattle were scattered. Most of them had a calf at their side or lying out in the sun nearby.

Bunched together just to his right, about a quarter-mile away, fourteen horses and two mules grazed peacefully. From time to time, one or other of the horses would raise a head and watch them, then return to grazing.

'Well, let's get 'er done,' Red said, nudging his horse forward.

He rode a circle around the small horse herd, positioning himself to drive them toward the ranch yard. When he was close enough that the herd began to move nervously, he called to his dog. 'Take 'em home, Pal.'

Instantly the dog exploded into action. He raced at the startled animals, as they began to move faster and faster away from him. As they began to move, he ran back and forth in a quarter circle, forcing them to run the way he wanted them to.

In minutes all were moving except the two mules. They had raised their heads to watch, then returned nonchalantly to the tall grass. The dog raced in on one mule, jumped and grabbed his tail, high enough to bite flesh instead of just the long hair. The mule instantly humped his back and began to lunge forward. Pal hung on, dangling from the animal's tail. He was safe from being kicked. As long as he held the tail, the animal would keep his back humped, rendering him incapable of kicking. As soon as he was moving the dog dropped off, dodging to one side swiftly to avoid the two-legged kick that lashed out as quickly as he released the tail. Without pausing, the dog sped to the other mule, performing the same feat again.

Convinced they had no choice except to go with the horses, the wise mules quickly caught up with the remuda. Rather than try to herd the horses, Red simply sat watching his dog work. He marveled, as he always did, at the dog's ability to know exactly what to do, to which animal, at precisely the right time, to keep them bunched and moving in the desired direction. He had little to do except ride along and watch the demonstration.

Pal was equally efficient with moving cattle, but totally refused to work with sheep. Because Red had bought him as a pup from a sheepherder, that had always puzzled him. He didn't run sheep on his place anyway, so it was no real concern.

Four hours later they came in sight of the barn. At once the herd picked up its pace, all heading as with one accord to the familiar environ. Only at the corral gate did they begin to balk and hesitate. It was the only time during the drive that Red and Useless had to help Pal actively with the herding. Together they quickly forced the animals through the gate. Immediately Pal sat down in the middle of the open gate, panting happily, daring any of the animals to try to get past him.

Red swung down and closed the gate. He patted the dog and rubbed his ears. 'Good job, boy!' he enthused.

Relieved of his responsibilities, the dog trotted to the water tank, drank thirstily, then lay down where he could watch and rest.

For the rest of the day Red worked with the animals. He dealt with the horses first. Each time he started to herd one into the barn, Pal would leap up, haze the horse through the door into the barn, then return to his resting place.

Once inside the barn, each horse acted as if he had been there only yesterday, walking immediately to the stall he was accustomed to, greedily munching the oats already in the feed box. Red went over each animal carefully. He curried and brushed the burrs from their hide. He worked the tangles and snarls from manes and tails. He checked legs and hoofs carefully, trimming their hoofs as he did. They were badly in need of being shod, to protect their hoofs from the rocky ground when they were being ridden or driven, but that would have to wait a day or two. He had a small forge just outside the barn door. He'd have the blacksmith come out from Lennox, since they all needed attention at the same time.

He left the mules until last. Unlike the horses, they didn't need to be driven into the barn. They had conceded their return to being domesticated as soon as they allowed themselves to be driven in with the horses. Red merely stepped to the door of the barn and called, 'C'mon Tyke.'

Instantly one mule turned and trotted across the corral, through the barn door, into his stall. He started munching his helping of oats at once.

Red stepped in beside the impressive animal. He stood fourteen hands at the withers, with a broad, full chest. Muscles rippled beneath the hide with every move. Red groomed him carefully, pleased to find him in excellent condition. He slipped a harness on him, then removed it again. Tyke didn't even flinch during the process. His stance projected total trust and complete acceptance of his role.

Leaving him in the stall, Red again stepped to the door. 'Your turn, Ike,' he called.

Ike responded exactly as Tyke had done. He was in as good a condition as Tyke, but had one small cut on his left foreleg. Red examined it carefully, cleaned it out, then filled it with a heavy, dark salve from a can he had procured in town.

As he examined the mule further, he thought he felt something wrong with his right ear. He ran his hand up along the mule's neck and reached a finger into the ear. The instant his finger touched the inside of the mule's ear, his left rear leg kicked violently. A bucket was sitting on the floor just behind, slightly to the side of the animal. When he kicked, he caught the bucket squarely. With a loud crash the bucket sailed into the air and smashed against the wall of the barn.

Tyke started at the sudden noise, but immediately went back to munching hay.

Red frowned. 'Never saw you do that before, Ike,' he said.

He stood facing the mule, just in front of his left shoulder. Tentatively he reached under the animal's neck, sliding his hand upward until he felt the right ear again. He scratched and rubbed the ear. Ike seemed only to enjoy the fondling.

Then Red reached a finger inside the ear. Instantly the left rear leg kicked violently again.

'Well, whatd'ya know?' Red marveled. 'Never heard of the like.'

Tentatively he stroked the left side of the mule's neck, working closer and closer to the left ear. When he had scratched and rubbed the ear for a full minute with no response, he reached a finger into the mule's ear. Ike responded only by shaking his head, then resumed eating.

Red again reached under his neck, and this time abruptly stuck his finger in the mule's right ear. Instantly the left leg kicked violently.

He shrugged his shoulders. He put the harness on Ike and removed it as he had done with Tyke. The mule acted as if it were a totally routine activity.

When he had finished, he released all but three of his horses from the corral. The others, along with the mules, he kept in the barn.

From then until darkness descended, he worked on his buckboard. He removed the wheels, one by one, greasing them, examining each spoke, assuring himself that all the wheels were tightly banded by the strip of iron around them.

Just before dark he walked down by the

creek, shot a rabbit, cleaned it swiftly and efficiently, and cooked it for his and Pal's supper. He went to bed pondering the strange threats Groon Kaiser had made. He knew their meaning would soon become evident, and it probably boded a fight to come. The dream of having all the fighting in his life behind him seemed suddenly quixotic.

He soon shifted his thoughts to Katy, and drifted off to sleep with a smile.

CHAPTER 7

Heads turned as the magnificent team of perfectly matched mules trotted into town. Red sat on the seat of the buckboard, looking relaxed and casual. Pal trotted behind the buckboard, acting as if the long separation from his master had never occurred. It was a perfectly normal picture of a rancher come to town for supplies.

The only detail belying that appearance was the second handgun. In addition to the Russian .44 tied down on his right hip, he now wore a short-barreled Navy Colt, butt forward, waist high on his left hip. It allowed him to draw as swiftly from a sitting position as his usual weapon allowed while standing.

In addition, a .44-.40 carbine lay handy to his right hand. It was no accident that all three of the weapons were capable of using the same ammunition.

Even more indicative of his caution, a double-barreled twelve gauge Greener shotgun lay within easy reach. He was shaken more by Kaiser's threats than he would have admitted. At least, whatever came, he was ready. Or so he thought.

He was not at all ready for what awaited him. As he trotted down the primary street of Lennox, he drew stares that were both friendly and openly hostile. Frowning, he tied up his team in front of the general store. He considered taking the shotgun with him, then decided against it. Instead he told Pal,

'Watch it, Pal.'

The dog instantly jumped up into the buckboard. He climbed onto the driver's seat, sat down and licked his lips a couple times. Ears perked forward, he sat there looking around as if he had just been crowned king of all he surveyed. Red knew nobody would approach the team or the mules while the dog was on guard.

He strode into the store, tipping his hat briefly to a lady who was just leaving. She looked at him strangely, but did not speak.

'Mornin', Cy,' Red greeted.

'Red,' Cy Fields replied. His voice was careful, guarded.

Frowning, Red asked, 'Things OK, Cy?'

'Yup. Fine.'

Red considered pressing. 'Glad to hear it,' he said instead.

He handed the shopkeeper a list of supplies. 'Got everything here?' he asked.

Cy glanced down the list. 'Yup. No problem. Want it loaded right away?'

Red looked at him closely. 'Any reason I'd

want it in a hurry?'

Cy was immediately uncomfortable. He cleared his throat. 'I, uh, just thought maybe you'd not be wantin' to stay in town longer'n necessary.'

'Why's that, Cy?'

'Oh, no reason. No reason at all.'

The store owner started to turn away, but Red laid a hand on his shoulder.

'There something I ought to know about, Cy?'

Cy glanced around, his eyes darting to all corners of the heavily stocked store. He cleared his throat again. 'I, uh, don't s'pose you've heard any o' the talk.'

'What talk?'

''Bout you an' the war.'

'Everybody knows I enlisted in the army and fought in the war. That's nothing new. What's the problem?'

'There's talk,' Cy evaded.

Exasperation edged Red's voice. 'Well, maybe it's time we stop talking circles and riddles, and tell me what's being said, and who's saying it.'

Cy took a deep breath. 'Don't like passin' on idle gossip,' he asserted. 'Still an' all, a man's got a right to know what's bein' said. There's talk that maybe you hid out durin' some o' the battles. That maybe you run when things got tough a time or two. Some hints that maybe you was sneakin' off from time to time to sell information to the Rebs. Stuff like that.'

Red's temper had risen, stage by stage, as Cy related the information. Anger quivered in his voice as he said, 'And anyone believes any of those things?'

Cy shrugged. 'You know how folks is, Red. They're awful quick, sometimes, to believe somethin' bad about most anybody. I ain't sayin' they believe it, either. Just wonderin', mostly, I 'spect.'

'Who's starting all those stories?' Red demanded.

Cy shrugged again. 'Don't rightly know. Everyone that's said anything to me has heard it from somebody different. Sorta like

81

shakin' a pillow out in a wind, and tryin' to figure out where all them feathers started out from.'

'Sounds like I maybe need to head upwind until I find out.'

'Easier said than done, Red.'

Red nodded in reluctant acknowledgment. 'Well, for whatever it's worth, there ain't one word of truth in anything you've heard. I got a bag o' medals and stuff from every battle I was in. I was trusted by every officer I served under. I never once betrayed that trust. And anybody that wants to dispute it, tell 'em to come say it to my face. Tell 'em to bring along two or three friends.'

'Doubt you'll get many takers to that one,' Cy replied. He smiled tightly. 'Most folks find it easier to talk behind your back.'

Red nodded ruefully. 'Seems that way. I'll stop over to The Waterhole for a bit, then be back.'

He considered again picking up the Greener from the buckboard, then changed his mind. No sense looking like he was itching for a fight. His irritation rose as he stepped through the doors of The Waterhole Saloon. He could hear the normal level of talk and laughter as he neared the door. He stepped through and paused, letting his eyes adjust to the dimmer light inside. The hum of conversation dropped steadily until the room was shrouded in an unnatural silence.

He could actually hear his boots crunch in the sawdust on the floor as he made his way to the bar. 'Short glass of your good stuff, Bub,' he told the bartender.

'Sure thing, Red,' Bub replied. His voice was affable, not at all guarded as the store-keeper's had been.

'Things going good?' Red asked, as Bub took his money.

Bub shrugged. Then he drove right to the point. 'You didn't make somebody mad, did you, Red? Some underhanded sort?'

Red pursed his lips. 'You might say that.'

'Wouldn'ta been a rancher that thinks he's king o' the universe, would it?'

'Could be.'

Bub nodded. 'Figured he was behind it. Seems like almost everyone in the last week or two has one thing on their mind. They been told by somebody that told somebody that heard from somebody that you was either a coward or a Confederate spy, or a just plain crook stealin' supplies and food from starvin' troops an' sellin' it ter get rich. The stories keep gettin' better by the day. Last count, near's I can tell, you stole pert-neart two million dollars' worth o' supplies, assassinated five Union officers an' four Confederate ones, raped fifteen or twenty women an' burned down half-a-dozen towns.'

Red didn't know whether to laugh or swear. He wondered how many would have the common sense of the bartender, put all the stories together, and realize they couldn't possibly all be true.

He sipped the whiskey, savoring the glow that spread through him as it settled in his stomach. The level of conversation in the saloon had resumed as he visited with Bub, but it remained somewhat subdued. The exception was the talk from a table where five cowboys had been drinking and playing cards. He had instantly recognized Billy Hand among the group. Wonder why he ain't glued to Kaiser's hip today, he mused to himself.

He didn't remember seeing any of the others at the table before. Aside from Hand, only one bore the telltale marks of a gunman. Their eyes were all still fixed on Red. Their conversations grew louder and louder.

Finally one of the group, a coarse-featured man who stood easily three inches over six feet, stood up and strolled across the room. Broad shoulders and lean hips telegraphed a great deal of strength and speed. He walked with an easy grace that added to his aura of power. Red watched his approach in the dirty mirror behind the bar. Not a man I'd prefer to pick a fight with, he told himself silently.

That decision was obviously already made for him. The big man stopped just to his left, eyeing him with a grin. 'Must take a lot of nerve to walk into a saloon with real men in it, if you're as much a coward as I've heard you are.'

Red didn't answer. The tide of anger rising within him since he drove into town was already dangerously near to overflowing. The word 'coward' surged it over the top.

Moving far too swiftly for anyone to respond, he whirled toward the speaker. As he turned, his right foot moved back to a position of maximum leverage. His right fist came up to shoulder level and shot forward. His body turned with it, focusing the full force of both his weight and his surprising strength on the fist that crashed into the big man's chin with an audible *thunk*.

He hit the ground hard, splaying sawdust from around him in a wide circle. He lay still for just a moment, as Red watched. His eyes flew open. He looked confused for an instant. He turned his head this way and that, then realized he was flat on his back on the floor. The saloon was deathly still.

He growled in surprise and anger, and rolled swiftly to his feet. Just as he gained his feet, Red's fist crashed into the big man's nose. Blood sprayed outward in all directions. He crashed to the floor again, knocking a chair reeling backward, where it was caught and righted by one of the men he had been sitting with.

With a roar the man sprang to his feet again, swiping the blood from his face, lunging toward the first man who'd ever knocked him down. It happened for a third time instantly, as a left hook from Red caught him squarely on the right cheekbone. His forward lunge veered sideways and continued until his face encountered the sawdust of the floor.

He rose more slowly that time, coming to his feet warily, eyeing this surprising adversary who should have been an easy mark. He came at Red swiftly, feinting with his right fist, then looping a wide left toward the side of Red's head.

Red rocked backward, letting the fist pass harmlessly in front of his face. He stepped quickly in behind it, sending first a left, then a right fist smashing into the man's abdomen. He was rewarded with a grunt at the first blow and a rush of breath surging out at the second.

Red stepped back and to the side instantly, barely avoiding two swift counter punches. Those punches left the big man slightly off balance, and Red took advantage by driving a hard right into his lower rib cage.

The quick-responding left from the man grazed the side of Red's head. Even though it was just a glancing blow, it made lights briefly flare in his head.

It also raised the level of his anger beyond the point of caution. He bore in on the big man, giving him no time to react or catch his balance. He sent a flurry of left, right, left, right, in what seemed an endless procession of hard, driving blows that rained first into his face, then his midsection, then back to his face, the sides of his head, his abdomen. As his antagonist began to reel backward, the pace of the blows slowed to allow Red to pack more power into them. After more than a dozen blows had found their mark, he stepped back for just an instant, then put everything he had into a right hook that caught the already staggering foe squarely on the jaw.

Red saw his eyes glaze over even before he toppled sideways. His shoulder caught the edge of one of the tables that had been hastily emptied on the way down. His weight tipped it and sent it skidding away on its side. The man landed heavily in the sawdust and lay without moving.

One of the cowboys who had been sitting at the same table with the defeated fighter swore and lunged to his feet. As he stood, his gun whipped out of its holster. As it leveled at Red, the gun that had leaped into Red's hand exploded, driving the would-be shooter backward. Rage, more than shock or pain, filled the man's eyes. He tried valiantly to raise his gun the rest of the way, but was driven back again by a second round from Red's .44.

'You boys get your hands on top of the table, where I can see 'em!' Red barked at the three remaining members of the original table. All three complied instantly. Billy Hand watched Red unblinkingly, a slight smile playing at the corner of his lips. His hands, Red noted, were soft, long-fingered, almost delicate-looking, even as large as they were. He reaffirmed his first assessment of the man. There's a man that won't face me, but I'd sure better watch my back.

'Anybody else here want to call me a coward or a traitor?' he demanded.

There were no takers.

Red spoke again, 'You can pass the word to whoever's spreading out all the lies about me, that if they have anything to say, they best come say it to my face. Anybody I even hear about passing on any of that bull will answer to me.'

He dropped his gun back into its holster, and turned back to the bar. Watching the room carefully in the streaked and cloudy mirror, he finished the remaining swallow of his drink. 'Sorry about the mess, Bub.'

'Don't worry 'bout it. I 'spect you'd best stop by the marshal's office, though. Tell 'im to talk to me if he wants your story backed up.'

'Thanks.'

With another careful look around the room, Red strode out the door.

He glared balefully up and down the street as he strode to the marshal's office. Small clouds of dust splayed up around his boots at every step. He stopped on the board sidewalk, took a deep breath, then opened the door.

'Mornin' Ben,' Red greeted the town marshal as he stepped into his office.

The marshal looked up then grinned broadly. He leaped from his chair and strode around the desk. He extended a hand. 'Red Denning! Heard you was back. Glad ya made it back in one piece.'

Red took the hand, gripping it gratefully. 'Thanks. Seems to be a few folks around that ain't real happy about it.'

Ben chuckled. 'Groon Kaiser comes t' mind real quick.'

'Him and anyone he can get to believe the

91

yarns he's spreading about me.'

Ben frowned. 'I've heard a few o' them. Can't imagine anyone believin' any of 'em. Leastways, nobody that's ever knowed ya.'

'You never know what people'll believe.'

'Yeah, I'm afraid that's true. So what brings ya by?'

'Just wanted to let you know I've had to shoot a man.'

'You shot a man? Here? Today? Who?'

Red shrugged. 'Don't have any idea. I stopped off at The Waterhole for a whiskey. Some fella picked a fight with me. Mentioned some of the stuff going around. Called me a coward, so I pasted him one. Danged if he didn't get up! Took me a little bit to get him whipped. Then one of his buddies jumped up and pulled a gun. Bub said to have you talk to him if you needed a witness.'

Ben watched Red closely, keeping his silence until he finished. Then he had a question or two. 'Who'd you whip?'

Red shrugged again. 'Never saw him before. Big fella. Probably six two or three.

Well put together. Yellow hair.'

'Are you kiddin' me? That's gotta be Leif Anderson. One of Kaiser's men. I don't think anyone's ever knocked Leif down, let alone whipped him. You ain't got a mark on ya!'

Red grinned. 'I didn't think it was a good idea to let him get started on me. He acted like he could pack a pretty good punch.'

'You ain't just a-woofin' he can pack a punch. Killed a man over east, I heard. Hit him just once.'

'I can believe it. What do you know about a guy that calls himself Billy Hand?'

Ben studied him carefully. 'Slender fella. Him an' Kaiser sorta been stayin' close enough together ya'd think they was joined at the hip. S'posed t' be hell on high red wheels with a gun. Ain't but one of 'is stories that's checked out at all.'

'You've checked on him.' It was more a statement than a question.

'Tried, anyway, when he first showed up. Brags a lot. Claims t've killed upwards o' twenty men. Only one I know he killed was down in Kansas.'

'Kansas?'

Ben nodded. 'He was a sure-'nuf gunman, too. Name of Frank Mobley. Hand shot him square in the heart.'

'Outdrew 'im?'

Ben frowned. 'Nobody was around t' watch it. Stubby Henson told me about it. He was with a bunch o' drovers that'd brung a herd up from Texas. He said Mobley was in the middle o' the road, more like he'd got shot off'n his horse than in a stand-up gun fight. Hole in 'im was puny big fer a pistol. But his gun was outa the holster, lyin' by 'is hand. Hand claimed he pulled leather on him, and there wasn't nobody t' naysay 'im.'

'Might have shot him from ambush with a rifle, then set it up to look legitimate, you mean?'

Ben shrugged. 'That's the idea I got from Stubby. It ain't somethin' I'd spread around, either way. Jist thought you'd oughta know you might watch your back.'

Red nodded. 'Do you know who's spread-in' all the stuff about me?'

Ben pursed his lips. 'Not much doubt where it's startin'. Not much of a way t' prove it, either, though.'

'Well, it'll likely die down on its own.'

'If it ain't bein' fanned.'

'Yeah. If. I got a load o' supplies down at Cy's, so I'll be headin' back out home if you don't have any more questions.'

'Go ahead. I'll get Reed to take care o' the one ya shot.'

Red drove the team home under a heavy cloud of impending trouble he knew he could not avoid.

CHAPTER 8

'I heard 'em, Pal.'

The dog had growled his usual warning that someone was approaching. Red had already caught the raucous protests of a pair of blue jays several minutes before. They had flown from someplace over the ridge, but their flight betrayed the passing of someone that had to be heading toward his place.

The day was bright and sunny. Red had brought the team of mules into the yard, and was putting the harnesses on them. When the jays had flown, he had stepped into the barn, picked up the double-barreled twelve gauge Greener, leaning it against a fence post just to his right.

He watched the direction the dog was looking, idly brushing Ike with a curry comb. Pat's hackles stood straight up along his back. A constant low, rumbling growl emanated from him in an almost constant murmur of warning. As he watched, three riders crested the ridge about 300 yards from where he stood. When they spotted him, they changed courses, riding directly toward him. They slowed to a walk, but continued on a direct course toward where he stood.

Twenty feet from him, they reined in their

horses and stepped down, as if on a pre-planned signal. Red had recognized one of the three immediately. Leif Anderson, Ben had said. His face showed the effects of that encounter. Both eyes were deeply discolored, one swollen nearly shut. His nose was puffed and red, pushed out of shape to one side. His entire face was swollen and bruised, lips three times their normal size. His movements betrayed the soreness of at least one broken rib and a lot more spots producing great pain.

The tall, lanky man to his right had also been in the saloon. Red had identified him immediately there as a gunfighter, but he had made no effort to interfere. He, like Billy Hand, had kept his hands carefully flat on top of the table and watched as one of his group was beaten unconscious and another killed. Now he watched Red with a far more sinister glint in his eyes. The one on the big man's left was smaller, and Red's mind instantly assessed him as the most dangerous of the three. He moved with nervous energy, but every movement bore the air of catlike grace.

'Mornin', boys,' Red greeted the trio, forcing his voice to be light, cheerful.

'Better'n yesterday,' Leif replied. His voice was thick and slurred by the swollen lips. 'Ya ain't gonna get a chance t' sucker punch me today.'

'As I remember, you were the one that started that party,' Red reminded him. As they had spoken, Leif's two companions had moved away from him to give themselves a clear line of fire to Red. He appeared not to notice, continuing to stroke Ike idly with the curry comb.

'I'm startin' it today too,' Leif asserted. 'An' it's gonna be a whole lot different this time around.'

Red smiled tightly. 'So you brought along a couple others to do what, Leif?'

'How'd ya know my name?'

Red ignored the question as well as the interruption. 'You decide you aren't man enough to take me on by yourself? Brought along a couple of your boss's hired guns to help? What's the play? Are they supposed to get the drop on me and let you beat on me a while, or are you just along to keep me busy long enough they can shoot me?'

'I don't need no help to pound you inta the ground,' Leif declared.

'Is that right? Then why'd you bring the help along with you?'

'You gonna fight me, or you gonna stand there playin' with that stupid mule?'

'Just waiting for you,' Red assured him. 'If you think you're tougher today than you were the other day, then come ahead and show me. Or do you need your baby-sitters to hold me down first?'

It was one more taunt than the already humiliated Leif could tolerate. Fists doubled at his sides he strode toward Red. Red reached his hand up along Ike's neck until he felt the base of the mule's ear. He waited, motionless, until Leif was positioned perfectly. He plunged his finger into Ike's ear. Instantly the mule's left hoof lifted and shot backward, catching Leif squarely in the chest with a muted crunching sound. The blow knocked him backward several feet, where he landed, spreadeagled on the ground.

Even as the mule's hoof was landing, Red was moving in a long dive. He grabbed the double-barreled Greener as he did, rolled to his feet gripping it at waist level.

Both gunmen were startled by the un-expected intervention of the mule into the equation. They recovered instantly, hands gripping guns that streaked upward.

That split second of distraction was enough. The first blast from Red's shotgun lifted the smaller man off his feet, doubling him up, propelling him backward.

So swiftly the sound blended with the first blast, Red emptied the other barrel at the taller gunman, even as the gunman's Colt fired. The Colt's slug passed Red's ear with an audible whine. The shotgun's pellets buried themselves in the gunman's upper chest and throat, knocking him backward.

The gunman caught his balance and fought

to bring his gun into line with Red. Red dropped the shotgun, his Russian .44 leaping into his hand. He held his fire, watching with grim fascination the fountain of blood from the gunman's torn carotid artery. Like an oil-lamp being turned down, the gunman's eyes faded, lost their glimmer, and went flat. He collapsed in a heap and did not move.

Red moved cautiously to where Leif still lay spread-eagled on the ground. One look at his face, mouth gaped open, eyes staring sightlessly into the air, was enough to confirm the mule's kick had killed him instantly.

Red holstered his gun and took a deep breath, exhaling it slowly. He looked around the yard, as if to find answers where he knew no answers awaited him.

He moved to his attackers' horses. Catching up their trailing reins, he led them to the corral, tying each of them to the fence. With great effort he hoisted the body of Anderson onto his shoulder, then lifted him onto his saddle, draping him face down across its seat. His horse edged and sidled nervously, but tolerated the burden. Breathing heavily, Red unfastened Leif's lariat from its leather strap. Using it, he lashed the body securely to the saddle.

He did the same in turn with the two gunmen. He started with the tall one first, saving the smaller, lighter man for last. When he had concluded lashing the macabre load to each animal, he untied them from the corral fence. Tying a knot in each set of reins, he hooked them over the saddle horns, where they would not impede the horses from their chosen course.

'Guess I'd just as well send 'em back to Kaiser,' he said. 'Let him know that plan didn't work either.'

He slapped one of the horses on the rump, to head it on its way. Instead of going toward Kaiser's Rafter K, it turned and trotted in the opposite direction. The other two horses swung into motion immediately, following the first one's lead.

Red watched with a puzzled frown until they were clear out of sight, still moving at a swift if nervous, purposeful trot. He shook his head and spoke to his dog. 'That's a surprise, Pal. I figured they were Rafter K horses, and they'd head straight for home. That one, at least, must've been that guy's own horse. Now it's headed back for wherever he came from.'

He thought about it for a minute, then chuckled. 'That just may not be a bad deal. Somebody, somewhere, is sure going to wonder where those three dead men came from. No telling how far they'll go before someone spots them and catches them. And Kaiser will just be left wondering what happened to the three he sent over here to get rid of me.'

He thought about it a few minutes longer, then grinned. He turned back to the almost harnessed team of mules. 'Nice day's work, Ike.'

CHAPTER 9

It wasn't clear how Red could drive the team effectively. Katy sat next to him on the seat, snuggled tightly against him, arm linked through his. From time to time she laid her head over on his shoulder for a while, then straightened again. She chattered happily as they left the Double-D-Bar. She was full of plans for the wedding, for things she wanted to buy for their home. She wanted to, as she put it, make their house 'show the proper hand of a woman.'

She was so excited to share her plans with him, she seldom waited for any response. As her first burst of enthusiasm expended, however, she began to notice his preoccupation.

She hadn't considered it that strange that he had helped her into the buggy on the left side, rather than the right. She was too excited at the prospect of spending the day with him to be that observant. Now she began to wonder about it. She noticed for the first time the carbine that lay against the seat at his right. She also belatedly noted the bulge on his left hip, where he did not usually carry a gun. Then she spotted the double-barreled Greener lying on the buggy's rear seat.

A gray cloud intruded its unwelcome shadow across her excited jubilance. She frowned, looking up into Red's face with troubled eyes.

'Is anything wrong, darling?'

'Wrong how?' he evaded.

'Wrong wrong,' she generalized. 'You're wearing two guns instead of one. You've got a shotgun on the back seat, a rifle in the front seat.'

'Observant little minx, aren't you?'

She ignored the jibe. 'I don't think you've heard a word I've said since you picked me up at home.'

'Sorry,' he apologized.

'You keep looking around like you expect

something to jump out at us,' she persisted.

'Didn't want to worry you.' It sounded lame, even to himself.

'So worry me,' she replied. 'We're going to be married. We're going to share our lives. You have to be able to tell me what's bothering you.'

'Not everybody's happy about us getting married,' he said.

She watched his face carefully. Furrows drew her eyes close together as she looked deeply within his. 'Groon?' she stated, more than asked.

'Gotta be.'

'Has he said anything to you?'

'Yeah. He stopped by the house the first week I was back. Told me you were his girl now, and he was going to marry you, and I had best move on before I had more trouble than I can handle.'

Her mouth dropped open. Her eyes widened. Fire flashed in their depths. 'Why that, that, that conceited ape! Whatever gave him the idea that I would be interested in him if he were the last man in Wyoming Territory?'

'Said he'd been seriously courting you. According to him, your pa is chomping at the bit to marry you off to him.'

Katy snorted derisively. 'He's tried hard enough to buy Father's favor. I'm embarrassed that Father accepted all the things he's been showering him with.'

Her voice took on an exaggerated gruff tone, trying to emulate Kaiser's voice and accent. 'Here, my good man, let me help you improve the blood lines of your herd. I have a hundred head of those red white-faced heifers that I really don't have as good a grass to support as you do. Let me give those to you...

'Oh, here, my friend, you really need to improve the general appearance of your buildings. I'm sure Cally and Katy would be delighted. Let me send some of my crew over while they have extra time on their hands. They'll rebuild those corrals and fences, spruce up the buildings, that sort of thing.

'My friend, as the man I hope will be my

father-in-law, let me have my men put on some of that wonderful new paint that the General Store has begun to stock. It will preserve the wood, and make your ranch an absolute showplace...

'Well, as friends and supporters of the Union, we must stand together. My marriage to your beautiful daughter would certainly be a great advantage socially and financially for you–'

'Piles it on pretty deep, sounds like,' Red interrupted the recitation.

As she had finally poured out the bottled resentment and irritation, she had visibly grown angrier and angrier. 'The pompous prig piles it on higher and faster than most men could with a manure fork!'

'Has he ever bothered you?' Red queried pointedly.

She shook her head. 'He's never had a chance! Mother and I have both seen to that. He's tried everything you can think of to get me alone. He even comes over every time he thinks Mother and Father will both be gone. I've made sure his sneaky tactics never work. I wouldn't be caught alone with him for anything.'

'Sounds like your ma shares your opinion.'

'She hates him with a passion,' Katy agreed.

'Odd your pa doesn't.'

Kitty sighed, leaning a head against his shoulder, hugging his arm more tightly. After a long pause she said, 'I don't really think Father likes him either. He's tried awfully hard to convince himself I'd be well off married to him. He likes being the recipient of Groon's generosity. I think, deep down, he's embarrassed by it. Belittled, as if he can't provide well enough for us without handouts from Groon. He didn't seem happy when you first came back, but he's really changed since.'

'Changed how?'

'Happier. Doesn't scowl and growl like a bear with a sore paw any more. He seems a lot more like his old self. He's planned to breed those heifers to our bulls, but yesterday he was toying with the idea of giving them back to Groon.'

'Might not be a bad idea. That'd serve notice he's not Groon's lackey.'

'So has he tried anything against you? Or were his threats more bluster?'

'He's tried,' Red said.

She picked up on the tautness in his voice at once. 'What happened?'

Briefly he told her of the confrontation in town, then of the one at his place.

'Oh, Red! Darling! They could have killed you!'

'That seemed to be their idea.'

'What are you going to do?'

'I'm not right sure. His sending his hired gunmen after me, I can handle; it's the talk I don't know how to deal with.'

'What talk?'

He took a deep breath before answering. His eyes never stopped their restless probing of the road ahead, every clump of brush and timber, every rise of ground that might accommodate a hidden rifleman. Finally he told her some of the talk that had been relayed to him. Her face reddened with anger, the color deepening with every accusation of the gossip he related.

'How in the world would anyone believe a single word of that?' she fumed.

He shrugged. 'I doubt if they do, really. But if somebody you know is a liar tells you the same lie over and over, it's hard not to believe at least part of it.

'If your brain's weak and feeble maybe,' she huffed.

He smiled tightly rather than answer. A few minutes later he said, 'Just kind of watch yourself while you're shopping. I'm going to stop off at the marshal's office. Bring him up to date. Then I'll kill some time at The Waterhole.'

'Just you make sure you kill time talking with the men in there, Marion Denning! Not with those floozies that ... that ... work there.'

He chuckled. 'Did I hear a slight note of jealousy?'

She harumphed with pretended offense.

'There's nothing there that I need to be jealous of. They have nothing to offer that I don't intend to smother and exhaust you with until you'll do well to be able to stand up!'

'Hmmm,' he grinned. 'Now there's a threat I fully intend to see carried out.'

She tilted her chin up and took on a tone to match the saucy look. 'All in good time, Mr. Denning. All in good time.'

'I could pull the team over there in those trees and we could get a head start,' he offered with a perfectly straight face.

She elbowed him hard in the ribs. 'You'll have more than you can handle, right after you put a ring on this finger.'

She held out her left hand, to show it empty of a ring.

He abruptly shoved a hand into his pocket and pulled out a large washer he had dropped in there while working on the buggy. He quickly slid it onto her ring finger, but its sides were too wide for it to fit between her other fingers farther than the second joint.

'OK,' he said. 'You've got a ring. Let's go.'

She giggled, elbowing him again. 'We're just going to town, mister.'

'That's sort of what I was thinking too. Really going to town.'

He reveled in the sound of her giggling yet again. Instead of elbowing him again, she just snuggled closer, hugging his arm with both of hers. 'If we weren't so close to town I just might be tempted,' she teased.

Unfortunately, they were that close to town, just entering its main street. He tied up the buggy in front of the Mountain Mercantile store. Looking up and down the street warily, he helped her out of the buggy. 'What time do you want me to show up again?' he asked.

'Meet me at the General Store at noon, and you can treat me to dinner at the café. Then I'll have some things picked out to show you at the mercantile.'

She tilted her face up for a goodbye kiss. He glanced up and down the street, then gave her a hurried peck, once again looking around to be sure he wasn't observed.

'Why Marion Denning,' she teased, 'are you embarrassed to be seen kissing your fiancée?'

Without waiting for an answer, she turned and walked into the store, her giggle trailing behind her.

With another glance up and down the length of the street, Red turned and strode to the marshal's office.

Humor danced in Ben Morgan's eyes as Red explained his disposition of the bodies of those who had sought to beat him to death or shoot him. 'Got a telegram from a sheriff in a place called North Platte, Nebraska. Seems three horses carryin' dead bodies wandered inta town. He was wirin' every lawman within three hundred miles, tryin' t' find out where they come from. Wired 'im back that they didn't fit a description of anyone that lives hereabouts. I 'spect they'll find a good spot t' bury 'em.'

'Must've been getting pretty ripe by the time they went that far.'

'I'd bet that sheriff smelt 'em afore he seen 'em, all right enough. Ya in town for long?'

Red shook his head. 'Probably longer than I want to be. Kitty ... Miss Dowling ... my fiancée ... is shopping for a bunch of stuff. She seems to think the house needs a woman's touch to make it more liveable before we're married.'

Ben chuckled. 'Well, you'd just as well go have a drink. You'll be waiting a while.'

Red nodded ruefully and left, walking across to The Waterhole Saloon.

'Mornin', Red,' the bartender greeted him. 'Whiskey?'

Red nodded. 'Short one, Bub. Kitty's shopping.'

Bub grinned. 'Maybe I'd best make it a double. You may be here a while.'

He moved on, but before Red could take a sip of the potent liquid, a man stepped up to the bar beside him, facing him rather than the bar. 'Your name wouldn't happen to be Denning, would it?'

Alarms sounded instantly in Red's mind,

but his face showed no reaction. Turning slightly to face the speaker, he casually switched hands, to hold the shot glass with his left hand. As he did, he allowed his right hand to drop to his side, just brushing the butt of his pistol.

'It would at that. That puts me at a disadvantage. Do I know you?'

'Not yet,' the man replied. His mouth smiled but his eyes remained expressionless, staring at Red. 'Name's Jack Sharp.'

He said the name as if he expected it to evoke both recognition and response. When it elicited neither, a brief frown crossed his face. 'Don't recall the name,' Red said, keeping his voice level and calm. 'Should I?'

The slender man shrugged. 'Thought ya mighta heard o' me. Folks hire me sometimes t' take care o' things for 'em.'

'That so? What kind of things?'

'People. People what are causin' someone problems. They hire me to t' take care of 'em.'

'You a doctor, are you?'

'Not exactly.'

Red pursed his lips. 'So let me guess. A fella named Groon Kaiser just happened to hire you to get me out of his hair, right?'

The slender man responded with a slow grin, revealing crooked teeth, darkly tobacco stained. 'I guess that's about the size of it. You wanta take care o' things right here, or outside?'

Instead of answering, Red whipped his shot glass in a quick arc. The contents were flung unerringly into both the gunman's eyes.

In the split second of Sharp's reaction to the burning sensation in his eyes, the barrel of Red's gun crashed against the left side of his head. He crumpled to the floor soundlessly.

Bub, the bartender, appeared behind the bar before the man's unconscious body settled into the sawdust. 'Not another one!' he complained.

'Getting downright tiresome, isn't it?' Red agreed, as if complaining about pesky flies.

Without waiting for a response, he bent

down to the insensate gunfighter. Grasping the trigger finger of his right hand, he bent it sharply backward. The motion was rewarded with an audible snap.

Bub winced at the sound. 'Ouch! That hurt, just listenin' to it. He ain't gonna be too happy 'bout that.'

'He's not going to try shooting anyone for a good while, either,' Red responded. 'Even after it heals, it may slow him up enough to make 'im find a different line of work.'

He pulled the gunfighter's gun from its holster, laying it on the bar. He checked his boot tops for a hideout gun, finding one holstered inside the top of his left boot. He tossed it on the bar with the other one.

He grabbed both the gunman's arms, slung him over his shoulder and carried him out the front door. Guessing the horse at the hitch rail bearing the Rafter K brand to be his, he flung him into the saddle. With his knife he cut a couple lengths from the virtually unused lariat fastened to the pommel of the saddle. One piece he used to lash the man's hands to the saddle horn. With the other he tied his feet beneath the horse's belly.

He walked back into the bar, oblivious to the small crowd gathering on the board sidewalk to watch.

'Do you have a piece of paper and a pencil, Bub?'

Bub's eyebrows rose in surprise, then lowered. He nodded then and walked through a door at the rear. He returned a moment later with the requested items.

Wordlessly Red took the paper, laid it on the bar, and wrote in a flowing hand, *Kaiser: The next man you hire to kill me better get the job done, or I'll consider it a necessary act of self-defense to send you to Hell forthwith.*

'How about a pin?' he asked Bub. 'Got one of those too?'

'I just wanted to sell you a drink,' Bub complained, 'not take ya t' raise.'

Red grinned. 'Humor me.'

Bub reached behind himself, removing the large pin that held the folded dish towel that served as an apron in place. He tossed it wordlessly on the bar.

Red picked it up, still grinning. 'I knew I could rely on a sophisticated bartender that even wears an apron.'

He walked out the door and pinned the note conspicuously on the unconscious gunman's shirt. Then he knotted the horse's reins around the saddle horn, led the animal to the middle of the road, and slapped him smartly on the rump.

To his surprise, three or four of the gathered and gawking crowd began clapping their hands in appreciation. At a loss for a way to respond, he waved awkwardly and turned to go find Kitty.

CHAPTER 10

Stories. Rumors. Whispers. Ephemeral things. Bodiless, invisible, impossible to grasp and throttle, but damning beyond any physical resistance.

The corral Red was busy repairing was receiving the brunt of his frustration. Post holes, chipped through intruding rocks with the long bar, then emptied of detritus and dirt, gave vent to only part of his pent-up rage.

Some of the stories being circulated were so ridiculous as to be laughable, were they not believed by at least some of those who heard them. The more outlandish included a rumor that he had betrayed his unit into a Confederate ambush that had resulted in their massacre. Another asserted that he had sold information to Confederate spies. Yet another claimed he had personally tried to assassinate General Grant.

Red had indeed returned from the war greatly enriched, but none of it achieved by nefarious means. He had led a small squad of men on one special, very classified and highly dangerous, mission. They intercepted a large, well-guarded shipment of gold, intended to procure supplies the rebel army desperately needed. The three surviving members of that squad had been rewarded with a portion of the wealth they had captured for the Union, as well as citations for their bravery. That, along with the carefully saved officer's salary, would enable him and Katy to build up the ranch and its herd.

He wondered if displaying the medals he had earned during his stint of service would dispel any of those rumors. Even as the thought passed through his mind he dismissed it. It would almost certainly be either derided as braggadocio or as stolen medals by those spreading the gossip.

There was one small benefit from the fuming, helpless rage that stormed within him. The post holes for the corral were certainly deeper, the posts tamped tighter, than they would otherwise have been. Part, at least, of his impotent rage dissipated with the sweat that soaked his shirt and ran down his face.

Pal's low, warning growl jerked him from the pounding of dirt and rage around a post. He quickly dried his hands on his pants' legs, and walked to where his rifle leaned against the corner of the corral fence.

Mere seconds later a hat and horse's ears appeared over the top of the rise west of the house. The rest of horse and man quickly rose into sight as well. A bright gleam of sunlight reflected from the left side of his chest. 'Lawman,' Red grunted. 'Not Ben, though. Looks like McReynolds.'

He set the rifle back down and walked out into the yard. The rider approached at a trot, stopping a dozen feet from Red.

'Mornin', Heck,' Red called. 'Get down and find some shade. Water in the trough for your horse.'

The man stepped wordlessly from the saddle. His bright eyes measured Red from beneath shaggy eyebrows. He pushed the front of his hat up, and spoke through the full moustache. 'A mite o' shade'd be welcome, Red. Champ'd sure enjoy a good drink too.'

'Mind if I have a look around your horse corral?' the sheriff asked abruptly.

Red frowned, 'Sure. Mind if I ask why?'

'Tell ya right shortly,' the sheriff replied. 'That all the horses you're usin'?'

'Two more and a team o' mules in the barn,' Red informed him.

McReynolds only grunted in response. He strode to the horse corral, opened the gate, and stepped inside. He walked around the corral for a few minutes, watching the horses as they moved in a group away from him. He watched the ground even more than he did the horses.

After a few minutes he walked into the barn. Red walked over and leaned against a corral post. He wished suddenly he hadn't promised Katy he'd quit smoking. Rolling and smoking a cigarette would sure help occupy his hands while he waited for whatever the sheriff was looking for.

Twisting the ends of his copious moustache, the sheriff walked out of the barn. 'Wouldn't have a drink o' water, would ya?'

'Sure thing. Bucket's right over there in the shade. Dipper's in it.'

The sheriff walked to the bucket. He took the long handled dipper, filled it with water, and turned a little way to one side. He drank thirstily, leaving less than half an inch of water in the dipper. He sloshed that bit of water around the dipper and flung it into the dirt, then returned the dipper to the bucket.

He walked back to Red. 'Don't s'pose you heard about the stage?'

Red frowned. 'No. What about it?'

'Got held up.'

Red's eyebrows raised. 'That so? Who by?'

'Not a clue,' the sheriff replied.

'What did they look like?'

'Only one set o' tracks.' The sheriff spat into the dirt. 'Don't even have a description to go on.'

'Why not?'

'He killed 'em all.'

Red leaned back against the corral post again. He folded his arms across his chest, studying the sheriff's face. 'All of 'em? How many?'

'Five.'

'Killed five people! What'd he get?'

The sheriff took a deep breath. 'Hard t' tell. Took one mail pouch. Took most ever'thing o' value outa everyone's pockets. Till we chase down next o' kin, we got no way to know what any of 'em was carryin'.'

Red's frown deepened. 'I don't get it. How could one man kill that many people, just like that?'

'Like a yellow-bellied coyote, that's how. I backtracked 'im. Seen where he waited, hid in the timber. Shot the lead horse to stop the stage. Then he stood there, hid, an' just gunned 'em all down. One passenger's six-gun had been fired four times. He was shoot-in' from behind the stage, but he wasn't no match fer a rifle in the trees.'

'Killed 'em all before he showed his face,' Red repeated, trying to digest the scope of the crime.

'Ya seen anybody strange ridin' by?'

Red shook his head. 'Nope. He head this way?'

'This general direction, afore I lost 'is trail on some rocky ground. Never could find it again.'

'No idea who, huh?'

'Nope. Only thing I know so far is half-a-dozen fellas it ain't. Includin' you, by the way.'

'How's that?'

'I'm a tracker,' the sheriff announced matter-of-factly. 'I'll know the horse when I find it. It ain't any o' yours. I didn't figure it was, but I had t' check.'

Red nodded, understanding why the sheriff wanted to check the corral and barn. It also explained why he had reverted to his normal demeanor as soon has he had done so. 'Well, it's nice to know I ain't guilty o' that at least.' He couldn't keep the bitter edge from his voice.

The sheriff's attention was piqued instantly. 'Some other things you are guilty of, is there?'

Red smiled tightly. 'Well, if you listen to some of the stuff being spread around, I'm guilty of about everything from double-crossing my outfit in the army to tryin' t' kill the President.'

The sheriff studied him carefully for several minutes before answering. 'Someone not happy about you bein' around, by chance?'

'You got the picture,' Red affirmed.

'That's hard t' fight,' the sheriff acknowledged. 'Well, at least we know you didn't rob the stage. You ain't no rustler, cuz it seems t' be your calves bein' long-roped. And if you're plannin' on shootin' the President, you're in the wrong territory. I think he's a ways east o' here.'

'Maybe I'm waiting for him to take a vacation.'

The sheriff abruptly changed the subject

again. 'One thing I can't figure, though.'

Red's eyebrows lifted. 'What's that?'

'I can't figure why the fella took one mail pouch.'

'One mail pouch?' Red echoed.

'One mail pouch.' the sheriff repeated. 'There was four of 'em on the stage. He'd rifled through all four. Strung the mail an' stuff on the ground. Did the same with the one he took. Then took the pouch.'

'Maybe he needed it to carry the other stuff he stole.'

The sheriff shook his head. 'Can't figure out anything he coulda got that wouldn't fit in a saddlebag. One o' the passengers mighta had a moneybelt full, but he wouldn't need a mail pouch for that. Now a mail pouch is a dead giveaway, if he's caught with it. Why take it with 'im?'

Red's face reflected the sheriff's puzzlement. 'Doesn't make a lot of sense.'

'Who's the next place up the valley?' the sheriff queried.

'Ralph and Theda Purcell have the next

place north.'

'Been there long?'

'Longer'n I've been here. Don't neighbor with them much, though.'

'That so? Why's that?'

'More of the war stuff. They're from Tennessee. Confederate supporters from the git-go. They don't have a lot of use for me, especially since I got the commission in the Union Army. Their daughter's got her cap set for Kaiser, but he's more interested in chasin' my girl.'

The sheriff's expression indicated that he understood the implications involved. 'If I come up needin' a deputy, temporary, kin I call on ya?'

'Well, yeah. Sure. Think you'll need help?'

The sheriff shrugged. 'Never know in this business. Nice to know who I kin holler at, if need be.'

With no further conversation, he walked to his horse, mounted, and rode out of the yard with a brief wave of his hand.

CHAPTER 11

When a woman fills a man's thoughts, other things tend to escape his notice.

Katy filled Red's, mind totally, this night. He wore his next best shirt and trousers, leaving the broadcloth suit he had determined not to wear until his wedding. His boots were carefully polished. Even the bright red neckerchief was brand new. His hat showed the results of careful cleaning and brushing.

Word had been passed from mouth to mouth about the big dance being hosted at the Dowling ranch. It was a combination barn dance and celebration of his engagement to Katy. People in that country lost no opportunity to socialize, or to celebrate. Life was hard. Its good times and joyous events were met with festive enthusiasm. Few within riding distance would be absent by the time the sun dropped behind the horizon.

A light breeze bore the scent of wild flowers. The westering sun smiled from an azure sky, that boasted half-a-dozen fleecy white clouds. Snow-capped mountains beyond the valley framed a picture of tranquil beauty that mirrored the joy of his thoughts.

Less than three weeks, now. Well, just barely over two weeks. Two weeks, and Katy would be Mrs Marion Denning. He smiled, his eyes distant, his mind filled with all the promise that prospect contained.

He rode a big sorrel gelding. Useless, the bay he usually rode, deserved a couple days' rest, so he had turned him out with hobbles that would prevent him from roaming too far.

The gelding was a good horse, but not quite as sure-footed and tireless as Useless. It was that one small difference that saved his life.

A mile and a half short of Dowling's Double-D-Bar, his horse stumbled. Red rocked forward, leaning for an instant across the saddle horn. At that same instant he felt a tug on his hat. A split second later the report of a rifle reached his ears.

Well-honed reflexes erased his preoccupation and launched his body into motion. He flopped from the saddle as if shot. He hit the ground hard. The air was driven from his lungs by the unyielding surface of the road. He lay still for half a second, then forced himself, still unable to suck air into his lungs, to roll over and plunge into the tall grass at the road's edge.

He crawled into the edges of a plum bush, loaded with white blossoms. Forcing himself to lie still, he quietly struggled to recover his wind. It took less than a minute.

He crept in a low squat far enough to see his horse. Bereft of its rider and confused, the animal stood in the center of the road. Reins trailed on the ground. As Red watched, his ears jerked erect. His head turned up the road.

In minutes Red spotted two men. On foot,

one sidled along each edge of the road, staying as close to cover as possible, craning their necks forward.

'You sure you hit 'im?' one queried the other in a hoarse whisper.

'Dang right I'm sure,' the other responded in the same whisper. 'Flopped like a poleaxed steer. He'll be lyin' right where he landed, with a hole right betwixt 'is eyes.'

'Shoulda gone fer the heart. Bigger target.'

'I ain't like you, I don't need a bigger target. At thet range, I kin light a match without knockin' the head off'n it.'

Red had a clear view of the duo now, from where he waited. Each wore a pistol, tied down. Each also carried a .30-.30 carbine, held loosely at their side. The picture they portrayed was an almost comical mixture of furtive caution and cocky confidence.

When they were about thirty feet away, at a place where no brush offered instant cover on either side of the road, Red stepped abruptly into the road.

'You boys looking for me?'

They both stopped in their tracks. Both mouths dropped open as if controlled by the same puppeteer's string. Both sets of eyes widened. Each stopped with a foot just touching the ground for the next step. No sound issued from either one. They stood as if frozen in time. For an instant, Red almost laughed. Then remembrance of why they were there erased all humor from his mind. 'Which one of you ruined my good hat?' he demanded.

He got his answer wordlessly. One of the men dropped his rifle. The gun was no more than an inch from his hand when he gripped the handle of his pistol. He swept it from its holster in a smooth blur of speed.

It is unlikely a man of his skill and practice would have missed a second time. Fast as he was, though, he wasn't fast enough. Red's .44 bellowed a roar of death, thrusting its ounce of lead into the gunman's heart, exploding it on impact.

His gun swung to cover the other gunman, whose gun was nearly clear of leather. That man swiftly changed his mind, letting the gun drop back into its holster. He raised his hands to chest level. He swore. 'I ain't never seen nobody thet fast. Chet was quicker'n anythin' I'd ever hoped t' see, an' ya got 'im cold.'

'Cold as you're going to be if you don't give me some answers quick.'

The gunman's head bobbed rapidly. 'Sure. Sure. Anythin' ya wanta know.'

'Who sent you to kill me?'

He hesitated only a heartbeat. 'Kaiser. It was Kaiser. Offered us two hundred fifty apiece. Said the last ones he sent after ya never come back, so don't take no chances. Chet, he never did like takin' chances anyway. "Shoot a man afore he even sees ya", Chet always said.'

'Works if you don't miss,' Red snapped.

'Didn't never see 'im miss afore,' the man complained.

Red said nothing for a long moment. The man began to fidget. 'You gonna kill me? If ya are, at least gimme a fair chance at my gun.'

Red holstered his gun. 'Your choice. Take your chance, or walk back to your horse and ride out of the country. If I see you again, I'll shoot you like I would a rabid dog.'

The man's head began to bob again. 'Thet's more'n fair. I'll sure do that. I will. I know I ain't no match fer you. I'm headin' back t' Texas, right now.'

He lowered his arms and turned. He began to walk away, without looking back. After four steps he whirled suddenly, his gun streaking upward.

Red was waiting for exactly that. His gun roared as the man whirled. The slug caught him in the chest, passing through his heart and both lungs. He was dead before he touched the road.

Red holstered his gun and stood where he was. He wanted to leave both would-be killers lie where they had fallen. Others would be coming along this road before long, though. Families, as well as single riders, would be heading for the shindig. It was certainly not a sight for children to see. It would just as certainly spoil the evening for most who stumbled across it.

He walked back to his horse and mounted. Riding back to the first body, he dismounted and looped his lariat around the man's feet. Stepping back into the saddle, he dallied the rope around the nubbin and nudged the horse toward the timber. When he had dragged the body far enough into the trees to be unnoticed from the road, he removed his rope. He rode back and did the same with the other body.

Coiling his lariat and replacing it in the strap that held it on the pommel of the saddle, he nudged the horse into a trot toward the Dowling ranch.

Katy was already surrounded by friends, neighbors and well-wishers. Even so, she saw him coming, as if she had been more watching for him than paying attention to them. She ran to meet him, flying into his arms as he dismounted.

She kissed him with fervor. 'Oh, Red, isn't this just too grand! Look at how many people are here already! And they all brought gifts! I thought it was just going to be a barn dance, but they've turned it into our engagement dance!'

'Did you think the most beautiful girl in the territory would get married without folks throwing a whingding?'

'Shindig,' she corrected. 'What's a whingding?'

He grinned. 'I have no idea. I think I just created the word. Sounds good, though.'

She wrinkled her nose at him, then reached up to kiss him again. 'I think everyone in the country is either here or coming,' she enthused.

'Everyone?'

Her eyes clouded briefly. 'Yes, he's here. I couldn't very well tell him to leave. He sure saw I wasn't happy he came. He said something that bothers me, though.'

'What's that?'

'He said ... oh, I can't remember his exact words. It was something about there might be even more reason to celebrate before the evening's over. What on earth did he mean, do you suppose?'

Red took a deep, thoughtful breath. He very much didn't want to rain on Katy's picnic. She was so excitedly beautiful. If she was this excited and beautiful tonight, he didn't dare think how wonderful she would look on her wedding day. He wasn't sure he'd be able to stand to look at her. Her beauty took his breath away already.

He knew he had to tell her, though. She had made him promise he wouldn't keep important things from her. He glanced around to be sure they weren't overheard. Gratefully he noticed that everyone was giving them a few moments of privacy to themselves. It wouldn't last long, he knew. 'I, uh...'

'Oh, Red! What's wrong?'

'Ran into a little trouble on the way over.'

'What? Who?'

'Two guys tried to bushwhack me.'

He took his hat off and showed it to her. Her eyes widened. She touched the hole in the crown of the hat with the tip of her finger. 'They, they, oh, Red! They just missed killing you!'

He nodded. 'If my horse hadn't stumbled, they would have.'

Tears began to stream down her face. 'Did they ... did you ... are they...?'

'They're dead,' he saved her having to ask it. 'But one of 'em told me who paid 'em. Two hundred fifty dollars apiece to kill me on the way here.'

'Was it...?'

Again he saved her having to ask. 'Groon Kaiser.'

'That bastard!' she exploded.

He laughed in spite of himself. 'Now where did my sweet, innocent fiancée learn to talk like that?'

She turned beet red. 'I'm sorry! I didn't mean to say that. But he... That... Are you sure they were telling the truth?'

He nodded. 'Stands to reason anyway. But I want to know how you know those kind of words.'

Her expression turned impish. 'You may

just be surprised at the things I know, Marion Denning. Just you wait a couple more weeks, and you'll really wonder!'

'Does my sweetheart have a secret past or something?'

She backhanded him in the stomach in feigned anger. 'No such thing and you know it. But I do have a very experienced mother who has seen fit to educate her daughter in the ways to keep a man satisfied and happy.'

'Well bless my soul,' he grinned. 'Maybe I should be chasing the mother.'

She expelled the pretense of an exasperated huff and hit him lightly in the stomach again. 'Why, I never...!'

Instantly, her eyes grew serious and troubled again. 'What are you going to do, honey?'

He stared at the throng of people just yards away. 'I gotta face him down and make him face me or leave.'

'Oh, honey! Please don't do anything to spoil everything. I mean... I'm sorry. That sounded terribly spoiled and selfish. But if you ... if he ... if somebody gets... If there's a gunfight, it'll be such a disaster for everyone.'

'Is that really what's worrying you?'

She looked into his eyes long and hard before she answered. 'Will you promise you won't hate me? Or be angry with me?'

He hesitated a long moment, leery of what she might be about to reveal. His love and trust swiftly overcame his misgivings. 'OK. Promise.'

She took a deep breath. 'I'm Irish, honey.'

'Yeah, I'd sorta noticed that a time or two. You've even got freckles...'

She hit him in mock anger again. 'Be serious!'

'Sorry.'

'You are not. Anyway, I know all the Irish superstitions are just ... just folklore. A lot of them didn't even come from Ireland. I know that. I don't really believe any of them. But it'd be hard not to worry.'

'Worry about what?' His confusion was becoming evident.

'There's just an old superstition that if

there's a major fight at your engagement party, you'll fight a lot with your husband. And...'

'And?'

'And if somebody gets killed at the party, one of us will be widowed within a year.'

'And you believe that?'

'No! No, I don't. At least I ... I don't think I do. But that was the first thing that popped into my head, when I knew you'd have to confront ... him.'

'So you'd worry, even if you don't believe it.'

'I'm sorry, Sweetheart! I don't think so. I don't know! I just don't want to have to find out.'

Their interlude of privacy'd been deemed long enough by the assembled friends and neighbors. Several people were walking toward them, clearly bent on returning her to the festivities. 'I'll try my best,' he said. He was rewarded by the rush of gratitude in her eyes, as she was pulled away by the half-dozen voices clamoring for her attention.

He skirted the small knot of people and headed for the barn. His eyes scanned the groups of people until he spotted Groon. Billy Hand was three feet from him as always, but he didn't see any others of Kaiser's crew. He was talking to the Purcells and Lester Forbes.

As he approached, Kaiser reached into his vest pocket and pulled out an ornate gold pocket watch. He opened the lid conspicuously, so those to whom he was talking could see the full circle of its ornate pattern. He checked the time, nodded his head, and tucked it back into his pocket. His hand brushed the white gold chain stretched across the vest, as if to assure himself everyone saw it as well.

The others saw Red's purposeful approach before Groon did. The glare he had fixed on Kaiser telegraphed trouble as clearly as the clarion tones of an alarm bell. Their conversation lulled in mid-sentence, and they began to back away.

Kaiser and Hand turned at the same time

to see the source of their sudden change of demeanor. Groon's eyes lighted on Red. His face blanched. His jaw dropped. His eyes widened. He looked as if one of the banshees from Dowling's superstitions had suddenly manifested before his eyes.

Billy Hand was just as visibly startled. He backed a step, clearly wanting to draw his weapon, and just as clearly afraid to do so.

'You look a little surprised, Groon. Didn't expect to see me here?'

'N-n-no!' He tried valiantly to recover his aplomb. 'I guess I am a little surprised to see you. I didn't see you ride up.'

'You must have been sure the two fellows you paid two hundred fifty dollars apiece to kill me would get the job done.'

Kaiser's eyes darted around, noting the rising interest in the confrontation. Others must surely have heard what Red had said.

Anger abruptly overwhelmed Kaiser's surprise and fear. 'How dare you come here making accusations! I could kill you for trying to ruin my reputation like that!'

'If you could kill me, you'd already have done it,' Red said. His voice was flat, hard as steel. 'Since you're not man enough, you've sent hired killers after me three times. Just because this is my fiancée's party and you're not worth ruining it for, I'll give you and your pasty-faced toady there exactly one minute to clear out of here. When you get home, you pack your stuff and get out of the country. If I see you again, I'll kill you on sight. Do you understand me, Kaiser?'

Kaiser opened his mouth several times to speak, but no sound came out. His hand reached toward his gun twice. Twice he thought better of it, and jerked it back away. He looked toward the gunman he had entrusted with his protection.

Billy Hand was keeping his hand carefully and obviously clear of his gun. As Kaiser looked at him, the gunman began to back away slowly.

Groon swore explosively and whirled away. He stomped toward the corral where his horse was tied, with the would-be gunman close behind him.

Nobody in Red's immediate vicinity spoke until the two had mounted and thundered out of the yard in a cloud of dust.

As if on cue, Pat Dowling's voice carried from the barn. 'There's some fine Irish whiskey in here, for any of you boys that'd care for a wee drop.'

Tension drained visibly from the gathering, and the sounds of celebration quickly resumed their normal pitch.

A deep twinge in Red's gut assured him that Groon Kaiser was neither willing nor capable of leaving the country as he had demanded. Both he and Kaiser were here to stay. One would ranch the ground he had staked claim to; the other would lie beneath it.

CHAPTER 12

It was a hard night's work. There was no rest in the near future.

Red was among the first to leave his and Katy's engagement celebration. Over her objections, he slipped away and rode swiftly to his own place.

He harnessed Ike and Tyke to the buckboard. Driving them at a swift trot, he left the yard in enough of a hurry to leave a dust cloud hovering in the moonlight marking his trail.

It was shortly after daylight when he tied up in front of a store in Rimrock. A sign across the false front announced, Lowenthal's Dry Goods and General Merchandise. In smaller letters beneath the name it boasted, Everything for Home and Ranch.

Inside, a small man greeted him, peering

at him over a pair of spectacles. 'You're out and about early this morning. What can I help you with?'

'Good morning,' Red responded. 'I'd like a case of dynamite, a coil of blackwick, twenty-five blasting caps, four boxes of .44 pistol cartridges, and four boxes of .44-.40 rifle cartridges.'

The storekeeper's eyebrows shot up. 'Not starting another war, are you?'

Red forced himself to chuckle casually. 'Not unless waging war on tree stumps, rocks and varmints qualifies. I've been gone the better part of two years, and stuff has sure gotten ahead of me.'

'Been off to the war?'

'Yeah, like too many others. At least I managed to come back.'

Hiram Lowenthal wasn't entirely satisfied. 'I don't believe I recognize you. Are you from around here close?'

Red shook his head. 'My place is in the valley along Cold Crick. I'm closer to Lennox than here, but Cy doesn't usually carry any blasting supplies. Seems to be a little nervous about dynamite.'

Hiram studied him for a long moment, then made his decision. 'Didn't know that about Fields,' he said. 'You wantin' it loaded right away?'

'Yeah, I'd like to head right back. If I let those mules rest too long they'll think they can take the rest of the day off.'

'Driving mules are you? I would too, if I were to be hauling dynamite. They're a whole lot less skittish than most horses.'

'They'll keep pulling a whole lot longer, too,' Red agreed. 'I drove that team two days and a night one time, without stopping for anything but water and an occasional bait of oats. They never flagged.'

'Is that so? Must be a fine team.'

'The best.'

The two swapped horse stories for half an hour. The store owner forked some hay onto the buckboard to cushion the dynamite. Then they loaded the explosives and a few other supplies. As he was about to leave,

151

Red's eyes fell on a bolt of calico material. 'Now that is some really pretty material.'

Lowenthal eyes opened a notch wider. He studied Red with obvious surprise. 'Women-folks have been favoring that pattern for curtains and tablecloths both, here of late.'

'I haven't seen any like it. I'm sure Katy would love it. I'll take, oh, about ... maybe ten yards of it.'

'Married man are you?'

He shook his head. 'Not yet. My wedding's just over two weeks away, though.'

'Well congratulations! How about if I throw in five yards of this gingham too, just as a small gift for the bride?'

Red started to climb into the seat of the buckboard when a noise from down the street arrested his attention. He stopped, one foot on a spoke of the front wheel, and watched.

'Just toss the clang thing up in the air, pilgrim. A hat like that's just beggin' t' be shot at. O' course, I ain't such a good shot, so I ain't likely t' hit it anyway.'

The speaker slouched in front of an impeccably dressed dude. His broadcloth suit fit him too well not to have been tailor made. The round bowler perched jauntily on his head was pure beaver, if Red was any judge.

The two who had him cornered were as opposite in appearance as would seem possible. From worn boots to bedraggled slouch hats, they were the picture of grimy personal neglect. Only the guns slung low on their hips showed any level of care and cleaning.

'I have no wish to enter an altercation with either of you,' the dude protested. 'Now please move aside and allow me to pass.'

Both of his antagonists burst into loud guffaws. 'Did you hear that, Lefty?'

In high-voiced mimicry he tried to echo the young man's New England accent. 'I have no wish to enter an alteration with either of you.'

'Altercation,' his companion grinned.

'What's a altercation?'

'It's a fight.'

'Oh! He don't wanta fight with us. That

what you mean, pilgrim?'

'That is precisely what I said, and I am not a pilgrim. Now please move aside and allow me to pass.'

Something about that struck the pair funny again. When they stopped looking at each other and laughing, one turned suddenly serious. 'Listen, ya walkin' mail-order pitcher, either ya take that hat off an' toss it up in the air, or I'll take it off'n you.'

'That would be most unwise,' the dude stated.

Muttering something incoherent, the speaker lunged forward. His hand reached for the brim of the young man's hat. As he did, his chin unexpectedly met with the dude's fist. He was sent sprawling back onto the board sidewalk.

He came to his feet amid a flurry of profanity. 'Why you tinhorn puppy dog, I'll tear you apart!'

As he bore forward toward his intended victim, the dude failed to notice the second man of the pair begin to circle around behind him. The move was not lost on Red. He stepped back into the street and walked rapidly toward the trio.

The greenhorn was proving surprisingly adept with his fists. His blocks and parries deflected every swing by his attacker. In contrast, he landed a steady succession of sharp jabs that quickly bloodied his opponent's face.

The forgotten opponent, however, had managed to get completely behind him. He drew his gun and lifted it, aiming for the perfectly round target of the bowler hat.

Just as the arm started its downward arc, his wrist was grasped suddenly in a grip of iron. Jerked off balance, he was whirled around just in time to take a ripping right hand angling upward into his midsection. Air exploded from his lungs. His gun dropped into the street from a suddenly limp hand.

Red knocked the hat from the man's head as he grabbed a handful of hair. Without allowing the would-be attacker an instant of respite, he jerked the man's head downward. His face met Red's rising knee with a sickening crunch. He collapsed instantly, out cold.

Red turned quickly to the fight in progress. The loss of his compatriot was not lost on the unkempt roughneck. He immediately stepped back and threw up both hands. 'All right, pilgrim,' he said.

His voice was suddenly conciliatory. 'No harm meant. We was just havin' fun. That's all.'

'Are you conceding?' the dude demanded.

'I don't even know what that means,' the ruffian responded. 'But I quit. I ain't fightin' no more.'

The greenhorn lowered his hands. 'Very well then. In the future you might consider more carefully whom you choose to challenge.'

It suddenly dawned on him that the man's friend was nowhere in sight. He turned around, and saw the one he sought unconscious in the street. His eyes darted to Red. 'What happened?'

Red grinned. 'He was going to try to see if he could bend his gun barrel over your head. I changed his mind.'

The dude's eyes jumped back and forth between Red and the unconscious man, until comprehension dawned on him. 'My word!' he exclaimed. 'And who might you be?'

Red grinned. 'I guess I might be most anyone. The name's Red Denning.'

The dude blinked twice, then grinned in response. 'Glad to meet you, Red Denning. My name is Brett Reese.'

'From Boston?'

The young man's eyebrows shot up. 'Why, yes! However did you know that?'

'Just from your accent.'

'Oh. I suppose it does sound rather strange in this environ.'

'Are you a peddler?'

'Oh, my, no–'

Red abruptly swept the young man out of the way, sending him sprawling into the dust of the street. In the same instant, his gun seemed to leap into his hand, barking death.

Twenty feet away, Reese's battered antagonist grunted and took a step backward. His gun slid from suddenly lifeless fingers. He followed it on to the street.

Reese climbed to his feet, looking aghast from Red to the dead assailant. 'What...? Why...?'

Red walked forward and kicked the man's gun well out of reach, should he prove not to be dead. It was an unnecessary precaution. He holstered his gun and turned to Reese. 'He waited until he thought neither of us was looking, then started to shoot you in the back. You got your suit all dirty. Sorry about that.'

Reese brushed himself off, scowling. 'He ... he tried to murder me?'

'That seems to be the idea.'

'And you suspected that he would.'

'It seemed likely.'

'My word!' he said once again, shaking his head.

'What did you say you're doing this far from Boston?'

Reese shook his head as if to clear it of incomprehensible events. 'I have come out here to find my father's murderer.'

'Your father's murderer?'

'Yes. He was killed some short time ago. I came as quickly as I received the telegram.'

'Killed, where? How?'

'He was murdered in a stage-coach robbery. Murdered and robbed, along with, I believe, everybody else that was on that stage-coach.'

'Ah. Down by Comb's Hill. Between here and Lennox.'

'You are aware of the incident!'

'Sheriff told me about it. Have you talked to him yet?'

'Not yet, but I certainly intend to do so forthwith.'

'Well, you'll have a chance forthwith. That's him.'

Reese looked in the direction Red indiated, just as Heck McReynolds made a cursory check of the dead man, then walked to them. 'Mornin', Denning,' he greeted.

'Who's the dead guy? What happened?'

As if in response, the assailant on the ground moaned and started to stir.

'These two fellas were razzing the dude,' Red explained. 'While he was fighting that one, this one slipped around behind him. He was about to knock him on the head with his gun barrel, when I stopped him. Evened up the odds a little. The other guy backed off then, waited till he thought we weren't watching anymore, and tried to shoot him in the back. I was still watching.'

McReynolds eyed him closely for a long moment, then turned to Reese. 'That how it happened, pilgrim?'

Reese's eyes flashed. 'I am getting rather tired of being labeled a pilgrim. My name is Brett Reese. And yes, that is precisely the proper order of events, most succinctly stated.'

Heck nodded. 'Yeah, that's the story Lowenthal told me, too.'

'His father was one of the people murdered in the stage holdup,' Red offered.

McReynolds studied the young man more closely. 'You come all the way out here to claim the body?'

'No. I have come to identify the murderer.'

'And just how do you intend to do that?'

'By an item he took from my father.'

'What sort of item?'

'My father always carried a very expensive gold pocket watch. It will be quite easy to identify.'

'Lots o' gold watches around.'

'Not like that one. It was unique in design. It is also uniquely engraved.'

'Engraved?'

'It has a message engraved inside the cover. It says, "To my Darling Husband" and the initials M.S.R. My mother's initials. The watch chain to which it was attached is equally striking and valuable. It is an alloy of gold and nickel, known as white gold. Quite rare.'

'He'd most likely get rid o' somethin' that odd. Too risky to keep it.'

Reese shook his head vigorously. 'I don't

think so, Sheriff. A person so enamored of money and finery as to murder that many people in cold blood, would be entirely incapable of discarding so beautiful and valuable a prize.'

The image of a striking, large, ornate watch chain crossed Red's mind instantly. He started to mention it, then thought better of it.

'I'll let you boys deal with that. If you don't have any more questions for me, Heck, I'll be heading back toward home.'

McReynolds looked at him a moment, nodded wordlessly, and returned to his discussion with Brett Reese.

Red drove out of town wondering if he'd been prudent or an idiot, to keep his thoughts and observations to himself. He mulled the idea the whole way home. He simply could not accept that Kaiser could be either that cold-blooded and calculating, or that stupid at the same time.

CHAPTER 13

Even in spring, the harsh sun leeched the energy from his body. It drew it out through every pore of his skin. It left him feeling as if he'd never reach home.

Twice he dozed off. Twice he was wakened by some unknown noise that prompted his whipping his gun from its holster, looking in all directions. Each time he holstered it again, feeling foolish.

Once he was dismayed to notice he had traveled over two miles since nodding off. He shook his head. He took a drink of the tepid water in his canteen.

At the next small stream they crossed, he paused to let the mules drink their fill. While they were at it, he did the same. The ice-cold water of the mountain stream restored some measure of his vigor, but not nearly enough.

His arms still felt leaden and slow.

He sloshed the icy liquid into his face. He removed his hat, filling it with water, then clapped it on his head swiftly, letting the intensely cold fluid drain down across his head and on to his shoulders.

The breeze through his soaked shirt made his flesh tingle. He suppressed a shiver, then climbed back onto the buckboard seat and started the mules on their way again.

It took him until late afternoon to get home. Ike and Tyke were showing the same fatigue he felt by the time they came in sight of his place. The mules picked up their pace perceptibly as the barn hove into view. Then he had to snap them smartly with the reins several times to persuade them to go on past home. He thought for a minute they were going to balk. With a good deal of persuasion they kept going, but showed their resentment the whole rest of the way. They pulled as if they were wading hock deep in mud. He couldn't ever remember having to push them that hard to keep them moving.

Another hour and a half later he approached a steep boulder-strewn talus slope. It slanted upward until it met a wall of solid granite. Above it the cliff rose vertically for 200 feet. Because of a bulge near the top, it was impossible for anyone at the top to even see the base of the cliff, let alone threaten someone taking refuge there.

He unhitched the team from the buckboard, leaving their harnesses in place. He led them back to a nearby bend of Cold Creek, picketing them where they had access to both good grass and water. Then he went to work.

For the rest of the afternoon he cut sections of the blackwick in various lengths. On the end of each he slipped a blasting cap, carefully crimping it with his teeth to keep it in place. Then he carefully inserted each cap well down into a stick of the dynamite. Using a roll of tough string, he wrapped coils around each stick, then around the wick, to eliminate any possibility of the wick and cap falling out, or being easily pulled out.

Half a dozen of the prepared dynamite had fuses nearly a hundred feet long. To each of these he fastened five more sticks of dynamite, tying them tightly together with the binding cord.

The clustered clumps of dynamite he placed strategically under and against large boulders. He fed each fuse carefully up the slope, keeping them down between rocks where they could not be seen. He arranged them in order at the base of the cliff, with the one leading to the farthest charge on one side, stepping down in order to the nearest charge on the other side.

The single sticks of prepared dynamite had fuses ranging from a few inches to a foot and a half. These he stacked almost against the base of the cliff. They were near the ends of the longer fuses, where they were both out of sight, and well protected from all directions.

He placed a box of matches, carefully wrapped in oiled paper, apart from the dynamite, but within easy reach of it.

Half of the stock of ammunition he had bought he carried up the rock-strewn slope as well. Huffing and puffing from the exertion, he wrapped it in oiled paper as well. He lay it beside the matches, weighted down with a flat rock.

Taking a tin of red pepper from his pocket, he poured it in a circle around matches and ammunition. 'That oughta keep the mice and such from munching themselves a big surprise,' he told his dog. The animal licked his lips and bobbed his head as if he understood every word.

When he had finished, he double checked the position of each cap in its respective stick of dynamite. He nodded once, and strode back to the buckboard. 'Bring Ike and Tyke, Pal,' he called.

His faithful dog sprinted away out of sight. In fifteen minutes he returned, gripping the mules' picket ropes in his teeth. The mules trotted obediently behind. Red hitched them to the buckboard again, and let them pick their own course home. They were more than willing to do so.

Aching with weariness, he stood in the yard after he had taken care of the mules. He was torn between the comfort of the house and the greater relative safety of bedding down in the trees behind it. Finally he said, 'Guard, Pal.'

He went into the house and collapsed on the bed. He was asleep in three minutes, confident his dog would warn him if anyone approached.

'Guess I'm about as ready as I can get,' he muttered as sleep overtook him.

His fitful sleep was marred by dreams of fuses that wouldn't light, the faces of friends appearing suddenly in his rifle sights, and snatches of battles past.

By daylight he was saddled and riding toward the Dowling ranch.

CHAPTER 14

A spring shower passed across the land, leaving it fresh, cleansed of dust and dirt. The clouds moved on, and the sun shone brightly. A light breeze stirred gently. Diamonds flashed from every small puddle. Birds sang, while big red fox squirrels chattered busily in the trees.

Red and Katy sat on the front porch at the Dowling ranch, holding hands, making plans. Their engagement party two days previous had been a resounding success, after Kaiser and his pet gunman had thundered out of the yard. They had heard nothing from him since.

They had, however, discussed at length who was, and was not, at the dance. The Purcells and Forbes, who had left shortly after Kaiser, were at least there briefly. Aside from them, they added up almost thirty able-bodied ranchers and homesteaders who had not been in attendance.

'Do you think they all believe any of those awful stories Groon has been spreading?' Katy had asked.

He had no answer that could offer any certainty. 'I'm sure a good number of them do,' was all he could say. 'More than likely most of them would just like to believe it. That'd give them a reason to try to run me out of the country.'

'There are far more people that believe in you,' she asserted.

He mulled the idea thoughtfully for a long while. She did not interrupt, content to sit beside him, hold his hand, and lean her head on his shoulder. From time to time she would lift the hand whose fingers were intertwined with hers, study it, trace his veins with the index finger of her other hand, then kiss it and lower it again. He seemed not to notice.

Finally he said, 'You're probably right. I

think most of the people in the valley know better than to believe any of his bull. At the same time, I seriously doubt that many of them believe in me strongly enough to come to my defense, if it should come to that.'

Her sharp intake of breath betrayed her consternation. 'You don't think Groon will try some kind of attack on you, do you?'

'Sure he will,' Red responded with absolute conviction. 'He doesn't have a choice.'

'Why doesn't he?'

'He isn't man enough to stand up to me by himself,' he explained. 'His pet gunfighter is no better. He's all fancy gunfighter clothes and big talk. I'd be really surprised if he's ever actually stood toe to toe with anybody in his life. He's dangerous enough, but he's a sneak killer at best. So Groon either has to drum up a lot of help, and try his best to kill me, or get out of the country, because he knows I will kill him. He has too much at stake here to run. He also has too much bluster and conceit. If he ran from me, he'd go crazy thinking about people knowing he

171

had done so. No, he has no choice. He will enlist as many as he can, on whatever pretext he can, and he will come after me.'

She stared into his eyes for a long time, trying in vain to find a crack in his logic. She could not. At last she said, 'When? How? Do you have any idea?'

'Soon,' was all he could think to say. 'It has to be soon. He will have to make his move before we're married. In his twisted mind, he probably still thinks he's got a chance with you, once he gets rid of me.'

'You've got to be kidding! He already has that Purcell hussy after him. Or so I've heard. How would he think I'd even look at him?'

'He doesn't think like a sane man,' Red insisted. 'He thinks he can always get his way, if he pushes hard enough, long enough, and pushes enough people out of his way.'

'And gets rid of you.'

'And gets rid of me.'

'Oh, Red. Darling. I'm afraid.'

Red's dog came abruptly to his feet. From beside Red's feet, he walked, stiff-legged, to the porch railing. The hair along his back stood on end. A low growl emitted from his throat.

'Rider coming,' Red said softly.

He released Katy's hand and stepped to the end of the porch. 'Best step inside till we find out who it is,' he said.

Fire flashed in her eyes. She opened her mouth to protest. Instead she whirled and flounced into the house. Before the approaching rider came into sight, she was back, however. In her right hand, hanging straight down at her side, she held a Colt .45.

Red hadn't even appeared to notice her return. She was surprised when he said, 'You still remember how to use that?'

It was the first time he could remember her snorting like that. 'I have practiced almost every day while you've been gone,' she informed him. Her voice sounded almost haughty. 'I would have thought you'd have at least bothered to ask.'

He resisted the urge to grin. 'I guess I was just too excited at our being together again,' he excused. 'How good are you with it?'

'I can shoot the head off a rattlesnake at ten paces every time,' she boasted.

His eyebrows arched. 'I am impressed, little lady.' She looked daggers at him. 'You call me "little lady" again and I'll practice on you! I am not a child!'

He chuckled. He deliberately and boldly looked her up and down. 'I am very, very much aware of that, my dear.'

'Here he comes,' she said. 'You don't act very nervous.'

He shook his head. 'Nobody to be afraid of, most likely, or he wouldn't be riding straight in by the road that way.'

'Oh.'

'It's Josh!'

'Who?'

'Josh. Josh Biddle.'

'I've never heard of him.'

'One of Kaiser's hands.'

'Oh.'

Hearing the tone of her response, he added quickly, 'But he's OK, Katy.'

'Did you know him in the war or something?'

'Nope. Met him after I got back. He was on the other side in the war.'

She gasped. 'He was a Confederate?'

'All the way through.'

'And you know him?'

'We've talked. He's come out and helped me work on the house a couple days.'

Further talk was interrupted by Josh riding into the yard. 'Hello the house,' he called out.

Red stepped out into the yard. 'Howdy, Josh. Get down an' come in.'

Josh turned his horse toward Red. When he approached the waiting man, he reined in and dismounted. 'I rode over t' your place, but ya wasn't thar,' he explained. 'Figured maybe I'd find ya here.'

Red noted the hurried tone of the man's voice, and his nervousness. 'Got time to sit a spell?'

Josh took a deep breath. 'I done quit Kaiser.'

'That so? Why'd you do that?'

Josh glanced around as if expecting to be overheard, or suddenly set upon by unseen foes. 'Kaiser's gone plumb nuts,' he opined. 'He rode over t' your place yestiddy. Took along Ralph Purcell and Les Forbes. Them an' big bad Billy Hand, o' course.' He spit out the last phrase as if it were a curse.

'Why did they go over to my place?'

'They said they was lookin' fer somthin', but wouldn't say what 'twas till they come back. They come back with a mail pouch what got stole off'n that thar stage what got robbed. Said they found it hid in a corner o' your barn.'

Pieces of an elusive puzzle began to snap together in Red's mind. 'That figures,' he said quietly.

'Glad it does t' you,' Josh said. 'It don't make no sense t' me.'

'The sheriff stopped by shortly after the robbery,' Red explained. 'One of the things he hadn't figured out from that robbery was why the robber would take one mail pouch with him. He dumped out everything that wasn't money, and left the other pouches.'

'Now that don't make no sense at all.'

'It does now. Kaiser's more devious than I gave him credit for. The stage robbery and the murder of five people in the process, was just part of a setup. He took the mail pouch so he could plant it in my barn, then pretend to find it.'

Words spewed explosively from Josh's mouth. 'Why thet no-good, back-stabbin', sonuva yellow-bellied, back-bitin' flea-bit prairie dog! Thet sneakin' slimy...What're ya gonna do now?'

'What's Kaiser got planned? Do you know?'

'Why he's a-roundin' up ever' one in the valley that'll pay any attention to 'im. Callin' 'em a vigilante posse. If'n he kin git enough of 'em t' suit 'im, they'll be ridin' straight fer your place, a-fixin' t' shoot ya on sight.'

'That's about what I expected.'

'So what're ya gonna do?'

'Well, I guess I'll ride over home and wait for 'em.'

'You're gonna what? Why, you ain't got a lick o' sense if you go doin' thet thar! There ain't no way ya kin stand up t' fifteen or twenty men!'

'You figure that's all he'll be able to muster?'

'Wall, thet's enough!'

'Time'll tell. Would you be willing to ride to Rimrock and let Sheriff McReynolds know what's happening?'

'Lotta good thet'll do! Ya'll be dead'n cold afore I kin get thar an' back.'

'Maybe not. I can hold them off for three or four days.'

'Three er four days? They'll jist burn ya out afore thet.'

'If I stayed in the house they would, sure. Do you know that big cliff north-west of my place? The spot where all the boulders and talus slopes up to the cliff, and it goes straight on up from there?'

'Sure. Rode past it a couple o' times.'

'I can get up there at the top of the slope, against the cliff. There's enough of an overhang nobody can go around to get above and shoot down or roll rocks down on me. There's a lot of cover. Even ricochets can't hit me as long as I stay in the right spot. The whole slope is in a clear field of fire, so nobody can get close. Even in the dark, that talus makes a lot of racket if you try walking on it. I can shoot at sound and stop anyone from sneaking up on me. I can keep a small army at bay indefinitely, as long as I don't go to sleep at the wrong time. I've got supplies stashed there to last several days.'

Josh studied him for a several moments. 'Sounds t' me like you've got this here figured out ahead o' time.'

'I knew it had to come. I just didn't know when, or what the pretext would be.'

'I knowed somethin' happened at the dance, t' other night. Him an' his pet bluster pup come home in a real lather. He was yellin' an hollerin' in the house so we could hear 'im clear out in the bunkhouse. Kept it up half the night. Madder'n a bobcat in a gunny sack, he was.'

'Bluster pup? I never heard that one before,' Red chuckled.

Josh snorted. 'Got a whole slew o' names what fits 'im better, thet I cain't use in the presence o' the lady here.'

'I can imagine,' Red grinned. 'But don't underestimate him. He's a dangerous man.'

'So long's he kin be behind ya, maybe,' Josh agreed. 'He'd sooner shoot a feller in the back than eat a square meal, if'n I got 'im pegged right. Then he kin claim another gunfight t' brag about.'

'I think you have him pegged,' Red agreed.

'Kin I git a fresh hoss?'

'Of course,' Katy interrupted. 'Take the big roan in the second stall. Take the iron gray next to him, too. You can lead one and ride the other. And hurry, Josh Biddle. You have to get the sheriff back here before they kill Red!'

'I do my dangedest,' he assured her, as he mounted and trotted toward the barn.

In minutes he thundered from the yard, riding one horse and leading the other.

'I gotta get goin',' Red mumbled.

'I'm coming with you,' Katy asserted.

'Not a chance!' Red responded instantly. His voice was flat and hard, leaving no opportunity or invitation for challenge or disagreement. 'I know you can shoot well, but I'm not going to have to worry about you being there too. Just be ready to round up some help if the sheriff needs it when he gets here.'

She opened her mouth several times to argue. Looking into the steely resolve in his eyes, she know it would be of no avail. Instead she rushed into his arms. 'Oh, Red, darling, be careful! Don't take any chances you don't have to. You have to stay alive for me. You have to!'

'I don't have any int–'

His words were cut off by her lips pressing hard, urgently upon his. In seconds her kisses transmitted more reasons for him to stay alive than an hour of promises could have done.

He just wasn't at all sure he would manage to do so.

CHAPTER 15

Katy stood in the yard, staring hard after Red long after he had gone. Her heart sank lower with every step of his horse. When he disappeared from sight, its ache turned to a physical throb. She stood transfixed by the horror of her thoughts until the last dust of his departure had settled.

A dozen thoughts tumbled over each other in her mind.

She could follow him, stand beside him, and fight to the death for the man she loved.

She could find Kaiser's posse, try to talk with them, reason with them, maybe shame them into abandoning their quest.

She could ride to the neighbors friendly to her or to Red. She could raise a posse of her own to ride to his defense. A range war would be better than losing the man she loved.

She could confront Kaiser herself, and try to shoot him. If she could succeed, maybe the rest would lose their resolve.

One by one she considered, then discarded, nearly a dozen wild, desperate plans.

Abruptly her chin lifted. The panic in her eyes was replaced with a hard resolve. She began to think, to plan, counting silently on her fingers.

She whirled and ran to the barn. Saddling her favorite horse, an Arabian gelding that could seemingly run forever, she sprinted from the barn.

'Go, Sultan! Run like the wind! Run like you've never run before!' she cried. Tears streamed down her face. She bent low over the horse's neck, unmindful of her tears dampening her horse's mane.

After the first quarter-mile, the horse settled into a rhythmic stride. The brush and grass beside the road was a blur. Up hills and down, his stride never faltered.

And hour and a half later she thundered into the yard of the Seven-Seven-Seven ranch. The dogs began to bark excitedly. Its owner, Wes Stevens, stepped out into the yard, shielding his eyes from the sun.

Katy brought the lathered horse to a stiff-legged stop. She tumbled from the saddle.

'Why, it's the Dowling girl,' he called over his shoulder.

He addressed the girl, 'What on earth is wrong, young 'un? Who's after you?'

'Mister Stevens, I need a horse, quickly! Your fastest Arabian.'

'Whoa, whoa,' the rancher insisted. 'What's goin' on?'

'Oh, Mr. Stevens! Groon Kaiser is raising a posse to kill Marion Denning, the man I'm going to marry. He's made all kinds of phony accusations, and framed him for murder, and said terrible things about him, and some of the Southern sympathizers are willing to help him because they don't like anyone who fought for the Union and if I don't get to Fort Connor quickly they'll kill him because even he can't hold out very long against that many people and he won't let me go help him and...'

Wes thrust a hand up in front of her face to stem the torrent of words. 'Whoa, little lady! Slow down a bit! Who are they tryin' t' kill?'

'Marion Denning. Red Denning. The man I'm going to marry.'

'He ranches in Cold Crick valley, don't 'e?'

'Yes, and they're trying to get rid of him because Groon wants me to marry him instead and I wouldn't marry him if he was the last man on earth. He's capable of absolutely anything and I know Red didn't do any of the things they're accusing him of–'

Wes held up his hand again, once more forcing Katy to stop for breath. Over his shoulder he yelled, 'Luther! Get Flyer outa the barn an' git this lady's saddle an' bridle on 'im. An' be quick about it.'

He turned back to Katy. 'Now you come over here an' sit on the stoop a minute, while Luther gits ya a change o' horses. Ya say you're headin' fer Fort Connor?'

She nodded vigorously. 'Yes. I'm sure the commander there will at least know of Red and his record of service and he'll know the horrible rumors are all a pack of lies that Groon has started just to try to turn people against him—'

Wes held up his hand again. 'You'd best save some o' thet breath fer ridin'. Come on over here t' the stoop. Ma's got somethin' fer ya t' drink.'

Katy sat down and accepted the glass of cool liquid gratefully. She gulped it down, then sprang up again as Luther began switching her saddle to a black Arabian mare. 'Oh, she's beautiful!' she exclaimed.

'She kin fly like the wind,' Wes boasted. 'None like 'er. Jist don't run 'er to death.'

'Oh, I already have it planned out,' Katy explained. 'I'm going to stop at the T-X Bar for another fresh horse. I've met Lance and Trudy Gilmore two or three times. They'll know who I am. Then I'll change horses once more at Gundersen's place, up past Rimrock. I've only met them once, but I'm sure they'll trust me with a fresh horse. That one will get me to Fort Connor.'

'Sounds like you've got it all figured purty good,' Wes acknowledged.

Katy handed her empty glass to Wes's wife. 'Thank you both, so very much. I'll bring your horse back and get Sultan just as soon as I can.'

Luther just finished saddling and bridling Flyer when she grasped the reins from him, sprang into the saddle, and bolted from the yard in a small cloud of dust.

Luther opened his mouth to speak as she approached, then stood there in silence, mouth open, watching her disappear north-ward down the road. His attention was brought back by Wes. 'Luther, quit yer gapin' an' git thet horse o' hers rubbed down an' walk 'im around some. Git 'im cooled down, then give 'im some water an' put 'im in a stall with some hay an' oats.'

Without ever saying a word, Luther moved to comply.

Almost two hours later Katy slid to a stop in the yard of the T-X Bar. Her conversation with Ted Gilmore sounded eerily like a repetition of the one with Hank Stevens. In fifteen minutes she raced out of that yard. At the fork in the road she bore north-eastward, toward the Gundersens' ranch.

Once again the exchange of horses followed, almost comically, a nearly verbatim echo of the previous two. Katy staggered as she dismounted, but gamely climbed into the saddle and left that yard at a dead run as well.

Approaching Fort Connor, she heard the sentry's shouted warning. Met in the gate by a weathered soldier sporting sergeant's stripes, she dismounted. Seven hours in the saddle, at a dead run, had taken their toll on her. As her feet hit the ground she staggered, and would have fallen if the sergeant hadn't grabbed her.

'Easy there, young lady,' he said. 'What's the all-fired hurry? Looks like you danged near run that horse to death.'

'I have to speak to the commanding officer at once,' she blurted. 'It's a matter of life and death.'

He studied her for several heartbeats,

glanced at her jaded horse again, and called over his shoulder. 'Corporal! Get this horse rubbed down and cooled off.'

A young soldier sprang to obey, eyeing Katy with open curiosity as he did so.

'Come this way,' the sergeant ordered.

Her first few steps were difficult and staggered. As she walked off the stiffness of too long in the saddle, her stride became more even, her steps longer.

She was led to a log building in the center of the stockade. It sported a plaque on the wall beside the door. 'Fort Connor, Wyoming Territory, Major Thom. Nielson, Commander.'

The sergeant opened the door. He motioned her inside, following her in and closing the door.

A corporal behind a desk looked up enquiringly. 'Young lady to see Major Nielson,' the sergeant announced crisply. 'Urgent.'

The corporal started to respond, then stopped. Something in the sergeant's eyes made him think better of enforcing regulations. Wordlessly he got up and went through a door into another room. He returned almost at once. 'Major Nielson'll see you now.'

The sergeant accompanied her into the room. 'Who are you, young lady?' were the first words out of the major's mouth.

He was every inch a military model, from his short hair, slightly gray at the temples, to the carefully trimmed white mustache. He stood ramrod straight behind a neat and perfectly arranged desk.

'My name is Katy Dowling,' Katy began. Speaking much more slowly than her instincts urged, she related the story she had rehearsed in her mind for more than seven hours.

Major Nielson did not interrupt until she had finished.

'Denning,' he said then. 'Major Marion Denning?'

'Yes, that's him,' Katy responded. The excitement put an edge on her words. 'Do you know him?'

'Know him! I served with him. I watched

that man ride that big bay of his through a hail of Confederate gunfire I doubted a sparrow could survive to pick up a wounded soldier and get him back to our lines. I have watched him receive more medals and commendations than I thought it was possible for one man to be awarded. Did you know he has even been awarded the Medal of Honor?'

'Is ... is that good?' Katy asked.

Major Nielson laughed suddenly and unexpectedly. 'Young lady, that is the highest honor the United States of America can confer on a soldier. Your fiancé is a bonafide hero!'

'Oh. Then ... then you will help him?'

'I would never live with myself if I didn't,' he replied.

He addressed the sergeant. 'Sergeant Winthrop, order a replacement mount for the young lady and have her saddle and bridle put on it. Order up 'A' company to be ready to ride in thirty minutes. Rations for two days. Order a supply wagon to follow and rendezvous with us at Cold Creek, five miles south of Lennox. Four-man escort with the supply wagon.'

Sergeant Winthrop saluted smartly. 'Yes sir,' he said. He turned on his heel and exited hastily.

Major Nielson turned to Katy. 'Now, young lady, may I escort you to the mess hall? You need something to eat and drink before we begin the ride. It will be necessary for us to stop in Rimrock *en route*. The army is not allowed to intervene in local law enforcement issues without the express request of an officer of the law. I'm sure Sheriff McReynolds will oblige, and if his acquaintance with Major Denning is such as you describe, I would expect him to accompany us as well.'

His expectations were accurate. Fifteen hours later they left Rimrock at quick trot pace. Both Sheriff McReynolds and Josh Biddle accompanied the unit. So also did three other deputies the sheriff had already enlisted for the purpose before the soldiers arrived.

Katy chafed at the pace, even though she knew it was as fast as a military unit could travel. They did not have the luxury of being able to wear out four horses on the trip.

Despair crowded the edges of her mind. Every time she calculated the time involved to get the help she had enlisted to rescue Red, it came out the same. She would be too late. They would all be too late. He could not possibly hold out alone against so many for so long.

Tears, unbidden, kept moistening her cheeks. Each time she swiped them away angrily. Each time they came again, as the miles seemed to drag by.

Major Nielson was both observant and solicitous. At one point he rode stirrup to stirrup with her for nearly a mile. Then he said, 'Ma'am, don't give up. I know Major Denning. It may well be his attackers who will be most in need of aid and succor by the time we arrive.'

She tried her best to smile through her tears. His concern touched her deeply. But even deeper was the growing conviction that her hopes and dreams were dying with the man she loved.

CHAPTER 16

Red didn't follow the road. Everybody allied against him knew full well how often he traveled the road between his house and Katy's. He had narrowly escaped one ambush; it was a foregone conclusion there would be more attempts.

He rode carefully. He constantly scanned the ridge tops, the trees, clumps of brush, rock outcroppings, any form of cover for sign of someone lying in wait.

When he topped the rise in view of his house he sat his horse in a clump of aspens for long moments, studying the scene. Even then, he wasn't sure he could trust his own senses. 'Scout the house, Pal,' he said.

Instantly his dog sprang into a full run. He circled the house and ran through the corrals. He leaped over the closed lower half of the barn door that opened into the corral and disappeared. Minutes later he reappeared, leaping over the door that opened into the yard. He trotted out to the middle of the yard and laid down. His tongue lolled out as he panted contentedly, watching his master who waited in the trees.

Nodding, Red trotted his horse down into the yard. He led him into the barn, and stood there thoughtfully for a long moment. He removed his saddle and put it on Useless. He put the bridle on him, but put the bit below his chin rather than in his mouth. He tied the reins in a knot and looped them over the saddle horn.

He got an old saddle from a tree by one of the stalls, and resaddled the mare he had been riding. He put a bridle on her from a row of bridles, halters and hackamores hanging at the end of the barn. He led the mare into the yard and called for his other horse. 'C'mon, Useless.'

Obediently, Useless followed him out of the barn. He stepped into the mare's saddle and rode off toward the cliff that marked the side of the valley, half a mile behind his house. Once more he called both the big gelding and his dog. 'C'mon Useless. C'mon Pal.'

Both horse and dog dropped in behind him as if they were tethered on lead ropes. Instead of riding directly toward the cliff, Red followed a line toward the north-western end of it, where it curved back to form one side of a deep canyon that cut far back into the mountain.

An hour later they came to a trickle of water flowing from someplace along the base of the cliff. Red stopped and sat there, listening carefully. After several minutes he looked around the clearing in which he sat. Lush grass reached above the horses' knees, even this early in the year. The trickle from the spring provided more than enough water. He turned and started to ride from the clearing, his dog staying two steps behind his mount.

Useless looked up from his eager munching of the tall grass as if determining whether to follow. Red called in a clear, sharp voice. 'Stay, Useless. Stay.'

Immediately the gelding dropped his head and resumed ripping off great mouthfuls of the inviting grass. Red trotted back toward the house. The dog followed. The horse stayed where he was. Returning to the house, Red left the mare saddled and ready in the barn. He and Pal repaired to the house to eat and wait.

They didn't have long to wait. The low rumble from Pal's throat was all the warning Red needed. He sprang from his chair, his meal little more than half eaten, and sprinted to the barn. Leading the mare outside, he sprang into the saddle. Just as he hit leather, a yell rose from the road, at the top of the rise approaching the yard. A dozen or more riders hove into view. Several more yells responded to the first. He could make out some of the words.

'There he is!'

'That's him!'

'Ride 'im down!'

The horsemen lashed their horses into a run, heading for him. Red clamped the spurs to the mare's sides, guiding her past the house, down the hill toward the creek. He was shielded from the approaching posse by the house until he was nearly to the creek. Just as he entered the brush and trees, several shots rang out behind him. Twigs and leaves scattered from trees above and around him. Most of the bullets were well wide of their mark. Just before wading the creek, he pulled his rifle from its scabbard and turned his horse sideways. Aiming through small gaps in the trees, he fired twice in rapid succession.

Two horses went down, spilling their riders over their heads onto the ground. The rest of the posse reined in abruptly, responding with a futile fusillade of rifle fire. By the time they did, Red had already turned the mare back and nudged her down into the icy waters of cold creek. At midstream he headed her upstream, taking advantage of heavy brush and trees along the creek bank.

He followed the stream far enough to make it appear he was trying to evade pursuit, then climbed the far bank. He chose a place to climb it that would leave telltale marks for them to find, but would not appear deliberate. Riding clear of the trees and brush that crowded the creek banks, he spurred the mare to a run, heading for a finger of scrub cedars that thrust itself out into the valley floor. As soon as he gained its protective cover, he dismounted. He hurried back to the edge of the cedars and settled down to watch.

There were obviously some accomplished trackers amongst his pursuers. They found his trail at once, and were following it fast. As they emerged onto the open ground between the creek and the cedars, they reined in. Two men were already riding double. They eyed the open ground warily. After a few minutes, one of the men cursed and spurred his horse forward. The others followed.

Red waited until the leader of the group was thirty yards from the cover, then aimed and fired. The man's hat flew from his head. He swore and jerked his horse around. Bending low over the saddle horn, he retreated to the cover of the creek bank at a dead run.

The others once again followed his lead. As they did, they once again sent a frantic burst of gunfire lancing into the cedars from where Red had fired. They riddled the brush he had hidden behind, but he was gone as quickly as he fired the shot. He ran to the mare, sprang into the saddle, and spurred her to action.

He bent low, holding his hat, to protect it and himself from the branches that lashed and tore at him as the mare picked her way swiftly through the dense cedars. Once again they broke into clear ground. On her own, the mare accelerated to a run. They crossed a flat outcropping of shale. The sound of her running hoofs on hard rock echoed back from the cliff, still well ahead of him.

That sound carried far enough some among the posse heard it. Red smiled grimly as he heard a chorus of yells well up from them. They knew he had fled, and they no longer need fear approaching the cedars.

Some of them spurred their horses to a run, riding right to flank the finger of cedars. Others forced their horses straight through, enduring the lashing of evergreen boughs, hoping to reach the far side while Red was still in range.

Some of them emerged in time to see him disappear into the brush along another loop of Cold Creek, 400 yards from the base of the slope that was his goal.

Once again a flurry of shots poked holes in the air and ripped foliage from branches, but nothing came close to him. At the foot of the talus slope he dismounted. He ripped the saddle-bags off, looped the horse's reins over the saddle horn, and slapped it smartly on the rump. As the mare trotted off, he climbed the loose and treacherous rocks as quickly as he could, saddle-bags in one hand, rifle in the other. Pal kept pace, scooting across the loose footing much more easily.

He was halfway up the slope when the first of his pursuers emerged from the trees.

They immediately sent a barrage of lead toward him. He was already, however, a lot higher than they, and farther away than it appeared. The slugs kicked up dust and ricocheted more than fifty yards from him.

Red stepped behind a boulder and dropped the saddle-bags. Taking into account the drop in elevation from his position to theirs, and knowing that gave his guns greater range, he aimed at one of Kaiser's hired gunfighters. An instant of silence followed the report of his rifle. Then the gunman clasped his chest, dropping his rifle. He looked up the slope in obvious confusion, then toppled forward. 'You boys are up against someone with way too much experience in too many battles,' Red muttered.

When the gunman collapsed, the rest of the posse stared in disbelief for a couple heartbeats. Then, as if someone had given a signal, they retreated into the cover along the creek. From the brush rifles barked a steady pattern, but none of them came close to Red's position.

He hoisted the saddle-bags and resumed his climb, all but daring them to try to hit him from that great a distance, up that far in elevation. He came to the top of the slope and stepped into the redoubt he had prepared. He glanced around quickly to ascertain that everything was in place and undisturbed. He sat down. Pal came and laid his head on Red's leg. Red scratched his ears and petted him absent-mindedly. 'Well, Pal, they aren't likely to try anything before dark. You watch, and I'll get some shut eye.'

With the ease of long practice, he dropped quickly off to sleep.

CHAPTER 17

The low growl woke him instantly. He lay still, listening. In a few moments he heard it too. Soft scuffing sounds came from the slope below. He guessed it was close to ten o'clock. The moon had set. Thick darkness shrouded everything. Figured they'd wait till the moon went down, he said silently.

He stretched, working the kinks out of his muscles. He stepped out to the edge of the downward slope. He cocked his head to one side, listening intently. Barely able to see the dog beside him, he studied the direction the animal was watching. As he did, the dog's head turned several degrees to the left. Then back to straight ahead. Then he looked a little way to the right. He kept moving his head that way, obviously picking up sounds only his ears could detect.

'Quieter than I thought they'd manage,' Red muttered.

Taking his cue from the dog, he aimed his rifle. He pictured the slope in his mind, adjusting the tilt of the barrel. Guessing how far up the slope his attackers had come, he began firing as swiftly as he could jack another cartridge into the chamber. As soon as the gun was empty he stepped back into the shelter of his redoubt, waiting for the responding hail of gunfire. No gun fired at the flash from his rifle barrel. Instead, bedlam broke out below. One man screamed, 'I'm hit!'

Boots on the unstable talus rattled in several directions. Together it made enough noise to drown out everything else that was said. He picked up snatches of loud cursing, shouted instructions, and angry responses. As if in answer to some hidden control, the noise died away. Eerie silence settled in its place. The stillness was broken only by a soft groaning from someplace down the slope.

'Must've hit one pretty good,' Red mused.

Voices began to disturb the empty silence of the night.

'...couldn't have seen what he was shootin' at.'

'Shootin' at sound.'

'Nobody kin shoot thet good jist at sound. Danged varmint kin see in the dark, I tell ya.'

The voice of Groon Kaiser rose unmistakably. 'Just be certain you keep him up there. We can smoke him out come daylight.

I have some things to attend to. I'll be back later.'

'We ain't tryin' t' sneak up thet slope agin,' one defiant voice declared.

'Just keep him cornered there,' Kaiser replied. 'He has no place to run. We can pick him off in daylight if he shows himself, or starve him out. He can't have carried any water up there with him.'

Several voices agreed. Two sets of hoof-beats retreated into the night.

'Gotta be Kaiser an' his pet,' Red muttered. 'Wonder what's so all-fired important for him?'

He was answered almost at once by voices that carried surprisingly far in the night's stillness. 'Where ya reckon he's a-goin'?'

'Home, o' course. He ain't gonna sleep out here on the ground like us.'

'I wouldn't neither, if'n I had what he's got awaitin' at home.'

'He ain't married.'

'Naw, but thet Purcell girl sure's sweet on 'im. She's been over there with 'im pertneart all the time lately.'

'Don't let Ralph hear ya say thet.'

'Ya think he don't know it?'

The answer was lost as the group moved back farther from the foot of the slope. Deciding there was little danger the rest of the night, Red laid down and went back to sleep. Before daylight he rose. He ate and drank from the stores he had secreted in advance, sharing both food and water with his dog.

At first light he was in position, rifle protruding between two boulders. From his vantage point he had a clear field of fire down the entire slope of boulder-strewn talus. Right at his feet were four fuses, a small pile of single dynamite sticks, fused and ready, and a supply of matches. With his knife he snipped a couple inches off the end of each fuse. He didn't want to have to fuss with a damp fuse end when he needed them.

The sun had not yet joined the daylight it sent ahead of it when the action began. Men began to scurry across the open space between the creek and the foot of the slope.

Silently, as if hoping he might still be asleep, they then crept from boulder to boulder, trying to work their way up the slope without exposing themselves.

Ralph Purcell started from behind a boulder, moving toward another. As he stepped from behind it, Red fired. His bullet struck a flat rock just in front of him, shattering it and ricocheting away with a sharp whine. Ralph swore and dived back behind the boulder.

Instantly several shots responded. Two rounds, from an excellent marksman, came perilously close to Red, bouncing off the rock just beside him.

He crouched lower and watched. Farther up the slope than he thought anyone had come, he caught a glimpse of one of Kaiser's gunfighters.

He bent over and picked up a single stick of dynamite. Striking a match, he lit the fuse. He watched it for an instant, to be sure it was burning. He stepped out from behind the boulder and heaved it in a high arc, ducking back as quickly as he threw it. Several shots pierced the air where he had been. From his cover he watched the dynamite arc up and back down. It just barely cleared the boulder behind which the gunman was hidden. It exploded the instant it disappeared.

Silence, except for the shower of rocks and skidding talus, followed the explosion. Then a dozen men began cursing at once. Red crouched down and lit the end of the longest fuse that lay at his feet. He yelled, 'You boys best get off that slope. The whole thing's going to come down on you.'

Deathly silence followed. Red could hear the angry hissing of the fuse as it sparked its way swiftly down the slope. 'That fella dead?' he heard somebody ask.

'Dang right 'e's dead,' another responded. 'Whatever he threw blowed up right beside 'im. Blowed 'im plumb in two, pertneart.'

Their conversation was cut short by a loud blast. Several sticks of dynamite, tucked beneath a large boulder, lifted it several inches, showering rocks and debris in all directions. The boulder, rocked from its resting place, immediately began to roll down the hill. It contacted lesser boulders, knocking them from their rest as well. In seconds, a large section of the slope was cascading downward with the deafening roar of countless rocks colliding with rocks.

Those in or near its path broke from their cover, fleeing as fast as they could, oblivious to their exposure to Red's fire, should he choose to shoot them as they retreated. Those not in line with the avalanche watched transfixed for several seconds. Almost as one they realized the rocks above them could well be in the same jeopardy.

As soon as the avalanche reached the bottom, expending its gravity-induced energy and rolling to a halt, Red called out, 'The rest of your boys best get off that slope too. There's enough dynamite planted there to bury you all.'

They didn't have to be told twice. They clamored from their hiding spots, sliding and rolling down the hill in their haste to escape. Once there, their courage began to return. They took up positions behind boulders at the foot of the slope, and began a steady barrage of fire at Red's shelter. He sat down where he knew he was safe from any ricocheting bullets, and waited.

From time to time he moved back to his vantage point and responded to the persistent gunfire. Once he caught Lester Forbes in the open and shot him in the leg. Another of Kaiser's hired gunfighters raised his head above a boulder at the wrong moment. He never felt the bullet from Red's rifle that ended his life.

The sun crawled to its apex, ignoring the life and death drama below. With agonizing slowness, it arced westward, finally turning its back on that part of the world. Darkness once again descended in its wake. At dark, while the moon was still three hours from setting, Red rose. 'C'mon, Pal,' he said softly.

Pocketing as much ammunition as he could, he worked his way back closer to the cliff. Just to the right of his redoubt about thirty feet, he squeezed behind a huge slab of granite that seemed to have broken away from the rest of the cliff. As he followed the narrow fissure, it began to widen slightly, and slope rapidly downward. With as little noise as possible he followed it for 200 yards. At that point it opened up, exposing a canyon. A shoulder of the cliff totally blocked its egress from where his attackers again settled down to wait for daylight.

He walked until he came to a trickle of water. He whistled a call that might've been some night bird. He waited a couple minutes and repeated it. In less than five minutes, accustomed to the moonlight, he saw Pal's ears prick forward. Shortly, from the direction the dog was looking, he could hear a tree branch brush against a saddle. Pal broke from Red's side, running toward the sound.

In less than a minute, horse and dog emerged from the trees together. 'Good boy,' Red praised the horse, scratching his ears and patting his neck.

He swung into the saddle and rode out,

skirting widely around those who thought he was still helplessly trapped at the base of the unscalable cliff.

CHAPTER 18

He heard them before he saw them. He reined Useless off the road into the trees. Waiting in silence, he glanced up at the sun, just peeking over the eastern hills.

'Whoever's coming must have been riding all night,' he guessed.

When the party came into sight, he almost fell from the saddle. Grinning broadly, he rode out into the middle of the road.

The large body of mounted men jerked their horses to a halt. Then one who was definitely not a man squealed in sudden delight. She spurred her horse, approaching him at a run. As her horse thundered past Red, she flung herself from the saddle, into his arms. He caught her, wrapping his arms around her in a burst of joy no less than hers.

'Oh, Red! You're alive! Oh! I was so afraid we'd be too late. It took so long to get to the fort and get everything organized and get all the way back and–'

She might have gone on that way a long time if his lips had not silenced her. By the time they parted, the party of horsemen had surrounded them. One of them led Katy's horse back, handing her the reins wordlessly. Red reached out a hand to the one in officer's uniform. 'Major Nielson. Long time no see.'

'Too long, Major Denning,' the officer responded, returning the tight handshake. 'You don't seem to be in dire straits.'

'Looks can be deceiving,' Red grinned. 'There's a dozen or more men back there who think they still have me cornered at the top of a talus slope.'

'Never choose a place to make a stand without a means of extrication,' the major intoned.

Sheriff Heck McReynolds interrupted.

'Josh Biddle tells me the riddle of the mail pouch has been solved.'

Red nodded. 'That and one other. I talked to a fellow in Rimrock the other day who's out here to find who killed his pa. He described a watch his father always wore. One of a kind. I remembered seeing that watch, but it took me a little while to make the connection.'

'You know who has my father's watch?' another voice broke in. A young man crowded his horse through the company, his face excited.

'Brett Reese, I believe,' Red recognized.

'You found my father's watch?' Brett repeated the question.

'I saw a man with it.'

'Who?' McReynolds demanded.

'Groon Kaiser. He was flashing it around, making sure everyone saw it, at our engagement dance, until I ran him off.'

'Then he is the man we must confront,' Reese asserted.

'That'd be the place t' start,' McReynolds

agreed. 'You know where he is, Denning?'

'Home, I'm guessing. He shows up where they had me under siege once in a while, but he doesn't stay there. I'm guessing he won't have left home yet today.'

Major Nielson spoke up. 'You don't need my entire company to arrest an individual.'

McReynolds agreed. 'Nope. Me'n Denning and Biddle an' the other three boys I brung with me kin handle that.'

'And me also,' Brett Reese injected.

'I would prefer that Biddle ride with us.' the major disagreed. 'He knows where this siege is under way. We will ride there, disarm and disperse those who have taken this quest upon themselves, and set them very straight regarding Major Denning's patriotism and military record. We will further inform them that Mr Kaiser is under arrest for robbery and murder. That should dispel any lingering loyalties that may influence them.'

Red felt a rush of gratitude that nearly left him speechless. 'I'm more than grateful, Major Nielson. Thank you.'

'Little enough in return for what you've done for your country,' he responded.

'That's not all, darling,' Katy enthused. 'Riding with us now are more than a dozen of your neighbors. They've heard about what Groon and the others are doing, and were riding to take your side. They ran into us a few miles back.'

Before Red could respond, Major Nielson turned to the sergeant at his side. 'Move the company forward, Sergeant.'

The sergeant barked the orders, while Red led the way toward the Rafter K. Katy rode at his side, close enough their stirrups kept bumping together. Neither seemed to mind. Half a dozen of his neighbors chose to ride with them as well.

As they approached the Rafter K yard, Red stopped. McReynolds took command. 'Ma'am, I'd like for you to light down over by thet tree. I don't want a lady in the way of gunfire. Frank, you ride around where you kin make sure nobody lights out the back door. The rest of you, fan out on either side

217

of us. Me'n Denning'll brace the house.'

Everyone did as bidden. Katy looked at first as if she would resist the order, but thought better of it and complied. When his men were in place, Red and Heck rode together to within twenty feet of the house. They dismounted, stepping a couple steps in front of their horses. 'Hello the house!' McReynolds barked.

A curtain pulled aside. A pale face of a young woman appeared briefly. In seconds the front door opened and Groon Kaiser walked out. Glancing around at the half-circle of men facing him, his face darkened. 'What's this?' he demanded. 'Who are all of you?'

He abruptly recognized Red. His face blanched, then darkened again. 'What are you doing here?' he demanded.

'My name is Sheriff Heck McReynolds,' Heck informed him. 'I have some questions to ask you.'

A movement at the corner of his eye caught Red's attention. He glanced up, just as a man on the roof of Kaiser's house, mostly shielded by the massive chimney, raised his rifle. Red's gun leaped into his hand, spouting fire. Billy Hand dropped the rifle and folded forward, rolling and tumbling down the roof. He toppled from the eaves and landed with an audible thud on the hard ground. He lay without moving.

Kaiser swore vehemently. Red holstered his gun. 'Groon, that's a fine-looking watch chain you've got. We'd like to take a look at the watch.'

'I don't have to show you anything,' Groon blustered.

'You can show it to us, or I will remove it from your dead body,' Brett Reese responded. His voice was flat and hard, totally different from anything Red had heard from him. He held an ornate Colt .41 pistol pointed squarely at Kaiser's chest. 'I'm willing to bet it has the engraving my mother had placed there for my father, followed by my mother's initials. Her initials were MSR. Does that ring a bell, Mr Kaiser?'

Kaiser's mouth dropped open. He closed and opened it several times. He swallowed hard. Brett stepped forward and jerked the watch from Groon's vest pocket with his left hand. He flipped open the cover and showed the inside of the cover to the sheriff. His eyes never left Kaiser. He addressed the sheriff. 'Sheriff, does that engraving say, *to My Darling Husband, MSR?*'

'That it does son. Groon Kaiser, you are under arrest for the murder and robbery of five men on the Lennox stage.'

Kaiser swore. From somewhere a gun appeared in his hand. He didn't get the chance to pull the trigger. Bullets from Brett Reese's gun, Red's gun, and two rifles from the men ranged out to make the arrest struck his body simultaneously. Kaiser's last curse died on his lips.

Several cowboys had come out of the cook shack. One of the deputies had swung around to keep them in view, but none showed any indication of interfering. McReynolds addressed them. 'Men, your boss has just been killed. Who is your foreman?'

One of the cowboys stepped forward. He was older than the rest. His mustache was more white than brown. Even the brown may have been more coffee and tobacco than youth. 'That'd be me. Charley Long.'

'Do you know of any family Kaiser has?'

Long nodded. 'He's got a sister in Cheyenne. I kin find her easy enough.'

'Then I will authorize you to take care of necessary business on this ranch until his heirs take control,' he said. 'Are there funds on the ranch to do that?'

'He's got a passel o' money in the house. Always does.'

'Then I will trust you to take charge of that as well.'

'Kin I kick thet floozie out as well?'

'Do so, and be sure she takes none of the ranch's money with her.'

The foreman only nodded. He walked toward the assembled crew by the cook shack. 'Shorty, saddle up the woman's horse. She'll be ridin' out in about ten minutes. You three Texas boys can come t' the house an' pick up your time. Yer done here. The rest o' you boys already got your orders fer the day. Get hoppin'. We got a ranch t' run here.'

He turned back to the house. Three of the crew, obvious gunmen rather than working cowboys, followed him. McReynolds spoke. 'Biddle, you an' a couple o' the boys tag along t' be sure he don't have no trouble with them hardcases.'

Biddle quickly pointed at Hank Wistrom and Al Folsum. The three dropped in behind the three gunmen and followed them into the house.

McReynolds turned to Red. 'Mr Denning, I believe somebody is waiting for you over by that tree yonder. May I congratulate you on your impending wedding, and wish you all the best.'

Red shook his hand and swung into the saddle. He kicked his horse into a gallop in his haste to rejoin Katy. He would never forget the feel of her body pressed against him in that embrace.

The publishers hope that this book has given you enjoyable reading. Large Print Books are especially designed to be as easy to see and hold as possible. If you wish a complete list of our books please ask at your local library or write directly to:

Dales Large Print Books
Magna House, Long Preston,
Skipton, North Yorkshire.
BD23 4ND

This Large Print Book, for people
who cannot read normal print,
is published under the auspices of
THE ULVERSCROFT FOUNDATION